THE SHADOW OF CONTROL

VIVEK RAGHUVANSHI

To those who dare to seek the truth,
Who refuse to be silenced,
And who find strength in both the light and the shadows.

This book is for the fighters—the ones who stand up, speak out,
and remain steadfast when the world tries to shape them into
something they're not.

And to every reader who has ever questioned, resisted, or refused
to back down: may you always find the courage to face the
unknown.

With gratitude,
The Authors

Contents

Foreword — vii

Preface — ix

Acknowledgements — xi

Prologue — xiii

1. Whispers In The Shadows — 1

2. The Architect's Web — 11

3. Crossing The Line — 20

4. Allies And Enemies — 30

5. The Depths Of Eclipse — 39

6. The Unseen War — 48

7. Breaking The Chains — 56

8. The Architect Revealed — 64

9. Fracturing Shadows — 72

10. A New Threat – Phoenix — 78

11. Rising From The Ashes — 84

Afterword — 89

Author's Note — 91

Glossary — 93

Foreword

In a world dominated by the rapid spread of information—and, just as often, misinformation—The Shadow of Control explores the power dynamics that shape our lives from the shadows. It is a story that delves into a world not too far removed from our own, where powerful forces seek to manipulate people through covert influence and subtle control. But, as this book shows, there will always be those who resist, who challenge, and who fight for the truth, no matter how high the stakes.

This story is more than a thriller; it's a journey into the delicate balance between freedom and control, individuality and conformity. Through the journey of Clara and her allies, we explore the resilience of the human spirit against forces that aim to undermine autonomy and reshape society from behind the scenes. The characters in this story grapple with difficult choices, conflicting loyalties, and a web of secrets that grows darker and more tangled with every step they take.

Writing this book was an attempt to ask some difficult questions about the nature of influence, the cost of freedom, and what it truly means to stand up against those who operate in the shadows. While The Shadow of Control is a fictional story, the themes are ones that resonate deeply in our increasingly complex world. The characters' battles may be set in a fictional landscape, but they echo real struggles faced by people across the globe, where courage, resilience, and integrity remain vital to preserving our humanity.

We invite you to dive into this story with an open mind and a curious heart. As you follow Clara's journey, may you find inspiration to ask questions, seek the truth, and—when necessary—be bold enough to challenge the powers that be.

With hope,

The Authors

40

Preface

When we began writing The Shadow of Control, we were compelled by the complexities of a world where technology, influence, and information intertwine in ways that are sometimes unseen, yet deeply impactful. Our inspiration came from observing how modern life is shaped by unseen forces—powerful institutions, influential individuals, and the algorithms that govern the flow of information. The story evolved from a single question: What would happen if a group of people decided not only to challenge those forces but to dismantle them from within?

At its heart, this book is about resilience. It's about standing up, even when the odds seem insurmountable, and about forging unlikely alliances when the stakes are highest. Our protagonist, Clara, finds herself thrust into a conflict she didn't seek but ultimately realizes she must confront. In the face of immense opposition, she learns that true power lies not in control or domination but in the courage to protect what is right.

Throughout the writing process, we were drawn to the duality of power—the seductive allure it has over those who wield it and the resistance it sparks among those who value their freedom. The Shadow of Control became a journey of discovery for us as well, as we navigated the layered complexities of loyalty, sacrifice, and the personal cost of seeking justice.

Our hope is that readers of this book will find themselves questioning and reflecting on the systems around them, wondering about the unseen forces that may shape their own choices. We invite you to look beneath the surface, to consider the quiet ways in which influence and control weave through our lives, and to ponder what it means to reclaim one's autonomy in an interconnected world.

The Shadow of Control is more than a thriller; it's a tribute to those who, despite the darkness, stand up to safeguard truth and integrity. We hope you find within these pages a story that challenges, excites, and, ultimately, inspires.

With gratitude,
The Authors
40

Acknowledgements

Writing The Shadow of Control was a journey we couldn't have completed alone, and we are deeply grateful to those who supported us every step of the way.

To our friends and family, thank you for your patience, encouragement, and understanding during the long hours we spent developing this story. Your belief in us and in this project gave us the courage to keep going, even when the road was uncertain.

We extend our heartfelt appreciation to our readers, both new and returning, who inspire us with their curiosity and passion. Your feedback, enthusiasm, and insights continue to motivate us to push boundaries and explore new themes. This book is for you, and we hope it resonates with you as much as it did with us.

A special thank you goes to our team of editors, whose dedication, keen eyes, and insightful suggestions brought out the very best in our story. Your expertise and commitment were invaluable in helping us refine and shape this book.

To the countless authors and creators who explore themes of power, resilience, and autonomy in their own work—you were our guides and our inspirations. Thank you for lighting the path and proving that stories have the power to challenge and change.

Finally, we wish to acknowledge everyone who, in real life, faces systems of control with courage and integrity. Your resilience and determination are testaments to the human spirit, and this book is a tribute to your strength.

Thank you all for being part of this journey.

With gratitude,

The Authors

Prologue

The storm began with a quiet pulse—a subtle shift in the flow of information, a whisper buried deep in the networks where power hid. Clara sensed it first, a feeling so faint she almost dismissed it. Yet, as the days turned into weeks, the feeling grew stronger, a knot tightening in her chest. She could see it in the news, in the headlines that seemed just a shade too polished, too carefully arranged. Something was coming.

As a journalist known for her relentless pursuit of the truth, Clara had seen her share of deception and manipulation. She knew the signs of influence, the trails left by those who believed they could rewrite reality to suit their agenda. But this was different. This was everywhere, a dark web of control spun so seamlessly it was almost invisible. And it had a name—the Eclipse.

The Eclipse was whispered about only in the shadows. Few knew its true extent, and even fewer dared to speak of it aloud. It was a power that moved through whispers, shaping the world with an invisible hand, weaving its influence into the highest echelons of society. No government, no institution, no one seemed immune.

Clara hadn't asked to be involved. She had planned to keep her head down, work her cases, and live a life removed from the tangled webs of the powerful. But now she was trapped in its shadow, hunted by forces she could barely understand. She had uncovered something that was never meant to see the light—a truth that threatened everything she knew, everything she believed.

The days that followed would test her resolve and draw her deeper into a world of secrets and lies. As the shadows closed in, Clara realized that she wasn't alone. Others like her, people she would come to trust with her life, were being drawn into this quiet war. They were the few who dared to stand against the invisible empire, the few who saw through the Eclipse's veil.

The path ahead was uncertain, shrouded in darkness. But as Clara took her first steps, she felt a fire ignite within her—a spark of defiance, a glimmer of hope. She knew now that some truths were worth risking everything for.

In the shadows, a storm was brewing. And Clara would be there to face it.

ONE

WHISPERS IN THE SHADOWS

Clara Hale jolted awake, drenched in cold sweat. Her heart pounded as she clawed her way out of the nightmare's hold, the lingering image of a darkened alley refusing to fade. She drew a shaky breath and glanced around, grounding herself in the familiarity of her small apartment. Books were stacked neatly on her desk, her work shoes sat beside the bed, and faint streetlight streamed through the blinds.

But the silence felt different tonight—thick, oppressive, like a presence lurking just outside her window.

She dragged herself to her feet, rubbing her temples to stave off the headache pounding behind her eyes. Sleep had become a fragile gift, one she barely experienced without a nightmare breaking in.

Her phone buzzed. A message from her best friend: Haven't seen you in weeks. Come out tonight?

Clara's fingers hovered over the reply. She wanted to say yes, to escape the gnawing sense of isolation, but she knew the dark, crowded spaces of the city's bars would only amplify her tension. Still, the thought of being alone gnawed at her. Maybe one drink, one small taste of something real, would ground her.

Be there in 20, she texted back, not allowing herself to second-guess the decision.

Pulling on a dark coat and her favorite scarf, Clara slipped out into the cool night. The city hummed with life, indifferent to her fears. But as she made her way through the shadowed streets, she couldn't shake the sensation that someone was watching her. Clara turned her head, catching only glimpses of strangers absorbed in their own lives.

But the feeling persisted, a prickling at the back of her neck. She forced herself to focus forward, each step taking her closer to her decision—and closer to him.

The bar was dimly lit, filled with the soft hum of chatter and clinking glasses. Clara slid onto a stool at the far end, keeping her back against the wall. She ordered a whiskey, letting its warmth seep through her as she scanned the room, soaking in the comforting anonymity.

But then, she felt it—that familiar sensation of eyes on her, cutting through the dim haze. Clara's gaze drifted to the corner, where a man sat alone, watching her. He was striking, with sharp features, a strong jawline, and eyes that seemed to hold a darkness of their own. When their eyes met, he didn't look away, nor did he smile. Instead, his stare held a certain intensity that made her pulse quicken.

He rose, moving through the crowd with a confident ease that suggested he was no stranger to places like this. In a few short strides, he was next to her, settling onto the stool beside hers.

"Mind if I join?" His voice was deep, carrying a warmth that contrasted with his intense gaze. He extended a hand. "Ethan."

Clara hesitated, but something about him—something in his eyes—drew her in. She took his hand, feeling the firm grip as he clasped hers. "Clara," she replied, her voice steady despite the strange rush of nerves in her stomach.

Ethan studied her, his gaze dipping from her face to the drink in her hand. "Whiskey. I wouldn't have guessed."

Clara raised an eyebrow. "What would you have guessed?"

He leaned back, a slight smirk playing at his lips. "White wine, maybe. Something soft."

She held his gaze, feeling a challenge in his words. "Guess you don't know me that well, then."

"Not yet," he replied, the words laced with intrigue.

They talked, slipping into an easy rhythm that surprised Clara. Ethan was quick-witted, his remarks edged with subtle humor, and he seemed to study her with a focus that made her feel both seen and unsettled. But there was something about him—a confidence that masked a layer she couldn't quite read.

"So, what brings you here alone?" he asked, his eyes narrowing slightly as he swirled his drink.

Clara hesitated, glancing down at her glass. "Sometimes... I just need a place to clear my head."

He nodded, as if he understood perfectly. "Sometimes it's the only place to find peace, isn't it? Surrounded by people but alone in your thoughts." His voice softened, and for a moment, his gaze held a flicker of something deeper—something almost haunted.

"Exactly," Clara replied, feeling an unexpected kinship in his words. "Though I have to admit, tonight I was trying to escape them."

Ethan's smirk faded, replaced by a serious look that made Clara feel strangely vulnerable. "From what?"

Her fingers tightened around her glass. She'd mastered the art of hiding behind words, of deflecting, but there was something about Ethan's directness that made lying feel pointless. "The past, mostly."

A silence settled between them, thick with unsaid things. Ethan's expression darkened slightly, as if he recognized something in her answer.

"I get that," he said, his voice barely above a whisper. "Sometimes the past has a way of following you, no matter how far you try to run."

Clara looked away, feeling a chill despite the warmth of the bar. She didn't know him, yet his words cut close to a truth she rarely allowed herself to face.

"Maybe that's why we're here," she murmured, almost to herself.

Clara watched as Ethan's expression shifted, his usual charm giving way to something more intense. His gaze lingered on her, penetrating, as if he were reading every unspoken thought. It made her feel exposed, vulnerable—but strangely alive.

"Tell me something about yourself," he said, leaning in. "Something you don't usually share."

Clara hesitated, feeling an uncharacteristic urge to be honest. Normally, she'd keep her walls up, but there was something about his voice, his presence, that made her want to let him in. "I don't...trust easily," she admitted, her voice barely a whisper.

Ethan nodded, as though he understood more than she'd said. "Sometimes, trust has to be earned."

She met his eyes, searching for the sincerity in his words. But in his gaze, she saw a flicker of something darker—a hint of a past that he, too, was trying to bury.

"Your turn," she said, trying to regain some control. "What are you hiding, Ethan?"

A shadow passed over his face, and he looked away, swirling his drink. "We all have things we wish we could forget," he replied softly. "Some memories are better left buried."

Days passed, and Clara found herself thinking about Ethan more than she intended. His words, his mysteriousness—they had seeped into her mind, blurring her usual sharp instincts. Against her better judgment, she agreed to meet him again, ignoring the warning bells echoing in her mind.

When they met at a small cafe, she felt the same intensity in his presence, an electric tension that both excited and unnerved her. Ethan leaned in close, and she noticed a scar on his hand, faint but jagged.

"What happened?" she asked, reaching out instinctively.

He withdrew his hand with a tight smile. "A reminder," he said, "of a mistake I won't make again."

The cryptic response unsettled her. Every time she thought she understood him, he shifted, revealing only enough to pull her deeper into his web. And yet, she felt powerless to resist, captivated by the shadows in his past as much as the man himself.

Clara had always been careful about letting people in. Her work as a forensic psychologist had shown her too many sides of humanity—some compassionate, others cruel, and a few disturbingly dark. But something about Ethan pulled at her defenses, making her feel both safe and vulnerable in ways she couldn't explain.

They met regularly over the next few weeks, each encounter drawing them deeper into each other's lives. Yet, every time she tried to ask him about his past, Ethan would deflect with practiced ease, turning the conversation back to her instead.

One evening, while they walked through a deserted city park, she tried again.

"Ethan," she said, stopping under a streetlamp that cast long shadows around them. "I feel like I barely know you."

He looked at her, his face half-hidden in shadow, and smiled that enigmatic smile that never quite reached his eyes. "Maybe there are parts of me you're not ready to know."

Clara's heart quickened, but she held her ground. "Maybe I am," she replied, her voice steady.

Ethan's gaze softened, but something dangerous flickered there, a darkness she hadn't seen before. "Curiosity can be dangerous, Clara," he murmured. "Sometimes it leads to places you can't come back from."

Her pulse pounded, her instincts screaming at her to walk away. But his words only drew her in further, like a moth to flame. There was a thrill in the danger, a part of her that wanted to see beyond the mask he wore.

"Then show me," she whispered, feeling a shiver run down her spine as she waited for his reply.

Ethan smiled, but his eyes held no warmth. "All right," he said softly. "But don't say I didn't warn you."

That night, Ethan took her to a side of the city she'd rarely ventured. The streets were quiet, the kind of quiet that felt more like a threat than peace. They walked in silence until they reached an old, unmarked building.

"Where are we?" Clara asked, eyeing the worn brick walls and darkened windows.

"A place from my past," he replied. "I thought it might help you understand me a bit more."

Clara followed him inside, her apprehension growing with every step. The interior was dimly lit, the air thick with dust and something else she couldn't quite place. Ethan led her down a narrow hallway lined with doors, each one closed, hiding whatever secrets lay within.

Finally, he stopped at one door and gestured for her to go ahead. "After you."

Clara hesitated but stepped inside, her curiosity overpowering her caution. The room was empty except for a table and a small stack of papers. As she approached, she saw that they were old photographs, faded with age.

Her breath caught as she picked up the top photo. It showed a man she recognized instantly—her ex, Daniel, in a photo she'd never seen before, looking younger and more innocent. Beneath it were more photos, showing him with other people, some strangers, some familiar.

Clara looked up at Ethan, her heart racing. "Why do you have these?"

Ethan's face was unreadable as he closed the door, locking them inside. "Because, Clara, I've known you longer than you think.

Clara had always been careful about letting people in. Her work as a forensic psychologist had shown her too many sides of humanity—some compassionate, others cruel, and a few disturbingly dark. But something about Ethan pulled at her defenses, making her feel both safe and vulnerable in ways she couldn't explain.

They met regularly over the next few weeks, each encounter drawing them deeper into each other's lives. Yet, every time she tried to ask him about his past, Ethan would deflect with practiced ease, turning the conversation back to her instead.

One evening, while they walked through a deserted city park, she tried again.

"Ethan," she said, stopping under a streetlamp that cast long shadows around them. "I feel like I barely know you."

He looked at her, his face half-hidden in shadow, and smiled that enigmatic smile that never quite reached his eyes. "Maybe there are parts of me you're not ready to know."

Clara's heart quickened, but she held her ground. "Maybe I am," she replied, her voice steady.

Ethan's gaze softened, but something dangerous flickered there, a darkness she hadn't seen before. "Curiosity can be dangerous, Clara," he murmured. "Sometimes it leads to places you can't come back from."

Her pulse pounded, her instincts screaming at her to walk away. But his words only drew her in further, like a moth to flame. There was a thrill in the danger, a part of her that wanted to see beyond the mask he wore.

"Then show me," she whispered, feeling a shiver run down her spine as she waited for his reply.

Ethan smiled, but his eyes held no warmth. "All right," he said softly. "But don't say I didn't warn you."

That night, Ethan took her to a side of the city she'd rarely ventured. The streets were quiet, the kind of quiet that felt more like a threat than peace. They walked in silence until they reached an old, unmarked building.

"Where are we?" Clara asked, eyeing the worn brick walls and darkened windows.

"A place from my past," he replied. "I thought it might help you understand me a bit more."

Clara followed him inside, her apprehension growing with every step. The interior was dimly lit, the air thick with dust and something else she couldn't quite place. Ethan led her down a narrow hallway lined with doors, each one closed, hiding whatever secrets lay within.

Finally, he stopped at one door and gestured for her to go ahead. "After you."

Clara hesitated but stepped inside, her curiosity overpowering her caution. The room was empty except for a table and a small stack of papers. As she approached, she saw that they were old photographs, faded with age.

Her breath caught as she picked up the top photo. It showed a man she recognized instantly—her ex, Daniel, in a photo she'd never seen before, looking younger and more innocent. Beneath it were more photos, showing him with other people, some strangers, some familiar.

Clara looked up at Ethan, her heart racing. "Why do you have these?"

Ethan's face was unreadable as he closed the door, locking them inside. "Because, Clara, I've known you longer than you think."

Clara felt the room close in around her, the weight of Ethan's words pressing on her like a physical force.

"What do you mean?" she whispered, her voice barely audible.

Ethan took a step closer, his gaze steady. "I knew Daniel," he said simply, as if that explained everything. "And I knew what he did to you."

A chill ran through Clara. Her past with Daniel was something she rarely spoke about, let alone to someone she had just met. "How? How could you possibly know that?"

Ethan's gaze softened, but it was laced with something unreadable. "Because, Clara, I was part of his life—until he crossed a line. I've been waiting for a way to make him pay, and that's what led me to you."

Clara's pulse hammered, her mind racing. She wanted to scream, to get away from this man who suddenly felt like a stranger. But part of her felt frozen, unable to tear herself from his gaze.

"You... you used me to get to him?" she asked, the hurt cutting deeper than she expected.

Ethan shook his head slowly. "It started that way. But it's different now." He reached for her hand, and despite herself, she let him, feeling the warmth of his touch even as she wanted to pull away.

"Why should I believe you?" she asked, her voice trembling.

"Because," he said softly, his fingers tightening around hers, "I'm the only one who knows what he really did to you."

A silence fell between them, heavy with things left unsaid. Clara wanted to pull away, to flee from this dark revelation, but Ethan's touch anchored her, his presence filling the empty spaces left by the memories she had buried.

"Tell me," she finally managed, her voice a mixture of fear and curiosity. "Tell me everything."

Ethan's gaze darkened, and he exhaled slowly. "It's not something you'll want to hear."

Clara steeled herself. "I need to know."

He nodded, leading her to sit on the edge of the table, still holding her hand as if afraid she might bolt. "I met Daniel years ago, before he met you. He was involved in some dangerous circles. I thought he was just another ambitious guy—until I saw what he was capable of."

Ethan's face twisted with a bitter smile. "People trusted him. They didn't see the monster lurking underneath, just waiting to show itself."

Clara felt her throat tighten. She had seen that monster firsthand, had barely escaped with her sanity intact. And now, here was Ethan, opening wounds she thought she'd healed. But his words made something inside her ache—a need to understand why fate had led her to him, to this moment.

"Why tell me this now?" she asked, barely holding back the tremor in her voice.

"Because," he replied, his gaze piercing, "if you're with me, you need to know everything. About Daniel, about me... and about the lengths I'm willing to go to protect you."

Clara sat in stunned silence, Ethan's words reverberating through her mind. The revelations about Daniel reopened old wounds, memories she had worked so hard to bury. But more than anything, it was Ethan's presence in her past—his connection to the darkest chapter of her life—that left her reeling.

"Why didn't you tell me sooner?" she asked, her voice barely above a whisper.

Ethan looked away, the faintest flicker of regret in his eyes. "I didn't know how. You were already so guarded, and I thought... I thought maybe it would be better if you didn't know."

Clara clenched her fists, her anger simmering beneath the surface. "So, what changed? Why now?"

"Because I couldn't keep lying to you," he replied softly. "You deserve the truth, Clara, even if it's painful."

She shook her head, feeling the weight of his words pressing down on her. "And what is the truth, Ethan? That you came into my life just to use me? That you were willing to manipulate me because of some vendetta against him?"

Ethan's face twisted with something that looked like pain. "It started that way, yes. But it's different now. You're different. I didn't expect... I didn't expect to feel this way about you."

Clara laughed bitterly, the sound hollow. "And what way is that, Ethan?"

He took a step closer, reaching out to touch her cheek, but she flinched, pulling away. "I care about you," he said, his voice low. "More than I thought possible."

She looked up at him, her heart a tumult of emotions—anger, fear, betrayal, and something else, something she couldn't bring herself to admit. "How am I supposed to believe you?" she whispered.

Ethan's expression softened, but his eyes remained shadowed. "I don't know. But I'll do whatever it takes to prove it to you."

TWO

THE ARCHITECT'S WEB

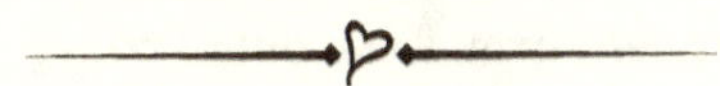

Over the next few days, Clara found herself wrestling with her emotions. Part of her wanted to cut Ethan out of her life completely, to rid herself of the pain his presence brought. But another part of her—a part she barely understood—felt inexplicably drawn to him, as though some invisible force tethered her to him.

She tried to go about her routine, focusing on work, distracting herself with friends, but Ethan's presence lingered, haunting her like a ghost. Every time she closed her eyes, she saw his face, heard his words, felt his touch. And despite everything, she couldn't deny the pull he had on her.

One evening, she found herself standing outside his apartment, her heart pounding as she raised her hand to knock. She hesitated, questioning her decision, but before she could turn away, the door opened.

Ethan stood there, his eyes widening in surprise. "Clara," he murmured, his voice soft with something that sounded like relief.

She swallowed, feeling her resolve waver. "I need answers, Ethan. Real answers."

He nodded, stepping aside to let her in. She entered, feeling a strange sense of deja vu as she looked around his apartment. It was neat, orderly, yet there were traces of him everywhere—the faint scent of his cologne, the books stacked neatly on the shelves, the photos lining the walls.

He gestured for her to sit, and she settled on the edge of the couch, her hands clasped tightly in her lap. Ethan sat across from her, his gaze steady, waiting for her to speak.

"Tell me everything," she said, her voice barely a whisper. "No more lies."

Ethan nodded, his face a mask of seriousness. "All right, Clara. But just know... the truth may be more than you're prepared for."

Ethan took a deep breath, his gaze fixed on the floor as he began to speak. "I met Daniel almost a decade ago. We were both working for the same investment firm, fresh out of college, full of ambition. At first, he seemed like any other guy—a little arrogant, but nothing out of the ordinary."

He paused, his eyes darkening as he continued. "But over time, I saw a different side of him. He was ruthless, willing to do whatever it took to get ahead. I started to suspect he was involved in some shady dealings, but I didn't have any proof. Then, one night, I found out the truth."

Clara leaned forward, her pulse quickening. "What truth?"

Ethan clenched his fists, his knuckles turning white. "He was blackmailing people. Manipulating them, threatening them, using their secrets against them to get what he wanted. And he was good at it—so good that no one ever suspected a thing."

Clara felt a chill run down her spine as she listened. This was a side of Daniel she had never known, a darkness she hadn't seen until it was too late.

"I tried to expose him," Ethan continued, his voice bitter. "But he was always one step ahead. Every time I got close to the truth, he would twist it, make me look like the bad guy. Eventually, he drove me out of the firm. I lost everything because of him—my career, my reputation, my friends."

Clara's heart ached as she looked at him, seeing the pain etched in his face. "And then you found out about me," she murmured.

Ethan nodded, his gaze meeting hers. "When I heard what he did to you... I couldn't just stand by. I wanted to protect you, Clara. Even if it meant using you to get to him."

Silence settled between them, thick and heavy. Clara searched his face, looking for any sign of deception, but all she saw was sincerity—a raw, unfiltered vulnerability that made her heart ache.

"So that's why you came into my life," she whispered. "Not because you cared, but because you wanted revenge."

Ethan's gaze softened, a look of regret crossing his face. "At first, yes. But it changed, Clara. Being with you, getting to know you... it wasn't part of the plan."

Clara shook her head, feeling a bitter laugh escape her lips. "But it didn't stop you, did it?"

He looked away, his jaw clenched. "No, it didn't. And I hate myself for that. But I can't change the past."

She felt a pang of anger, a surge of frustration that he could so easily admit his wrongdoing and expect forgiveness. "What am I supposed to do with that, Ethan? How am I supposed to move on from this?"

He reached for her hand, his touch warm and steady. "I don't know," he said softly. "But I want to try, if you'll let me. I want to be someone you can trust, someone you don't have to fear."

Clara felt tears prick her eyes, a mixture of anger, sadness, and something she couldn't quite name. She wanted to believe him, wanted to trust that he could be different, that he could be the man he claimed to be. But her heart was wary, scarred by the betrayal she had endured.

"I don't know if I can," she whispered, pulling her hand away.

Ethan's face fell, but he nodded, a look of resignation in his eyes. "I understand."

Clara left Ethan's apartment that night, her mind a whirlwind of emotions. She had come seeking answers, and she had found them—but they had only left her more confused, more uncertain about her feelings.

In the days that followed, she tried to distance herself, to put space between them and the tangled mess of their relationship. But no matter how hard she tried, she couldn't shake the memories, couldn't forget the way he had looked at her, the way his touch had made her feel.

One evening, as she sat alone in her apartment, her phone buzzed. It was a message from Ethan: I'm sorry for everything. I'll leave you alone if that's what you want, but please know... I never meant to hurt you.

Clara stared at the message, her heart pounding. Part of her wanted to ignore it, to let him fade into her past. But another part of her—a part she barely understood—wanted to reach out, to see if there was a way forward.

Taking a deep breath, she typed a reply: I don't know what I want. But maybe we can talk?

His response was almost immediate: Anytime, anywhere.

They agreed to meet at a quiet park, away from the noise of the city, where they could talk without distractions. As she approached, she saw him waiting by a bench, his hands tucked into his pockets, his face a mask of quiet anticipation.

He looked up as she neared, his gaze meeting hers with a mixture of hope and trepidation. "Clara," he murmured, his voice soft.

She sat beside him, her heart pounding, unsure of where to begin. "I don't know if I can ever forgive you," she said finally, her voice steady but laced with emotion. "But I need to understand why. Why would you put me through this?"

Ethan's expression softened, and he looked away, his gaze distant. "Because I didn't know how else to fight my demons. And then you came into my life, and everything changed."

Clara's heart clenched at Ethan's words, a mix of empathy and anger twisting inside her. She could see the pain etched into his features, the years of bitterness and regret that had led him here. But could she really forgive him? Could she truly let him back into her life after everything?

"Ethan," she began, searching for the right words, "I know you've been through things I can't even imagine. But I was dragged into this without a choice. I trusted you, and you... you used that."

He nodded, the remorse clear in his eyes. "I know. And there's nothing I can say to change that, Clara. I wish I could undo everything, but I can't. All I can do now is be honest with you."

She looked away, staring at the trees swaying gently in the evening breeze. "How do I know this isn't just another manipulation?"

Ethan's voice was steady, yet heavy with vulnerability. "I have nothing left to gain, Clara. If I lose you, I lose everything. That's why I'm willing to be here, to answer every question you have, even if it means reliving things I'd rather forget."

There was a silence between them as Clara processed his words, her heart and mind warring within her. She had been so sure of her anger, her resolve to shut him out. But sitting here, listening to him, she felt her defenses begin to crumble.

"You want me to believe you've changed," she said quietly. "But can you understand why that's so hard for me?"

He reached out, hesitating before his hand settled gently over hers. "I understand more than you know," he murmured. "But I'm here, and I'll wait as long as it takes. You deserve someone who won't run, who won't lie. And I want to be that person for you, Clara."

The days that followed were a blur of cautious reconnections and tentative conversations. Clara found herself slowly allowing Ethan back into her life, one small step at a time. He was patient, never pushing, always respectful of the boundaries she set. And, to her surprise, she found herself drawn to him in ways she couldn't quite explain.

One evening, they met at a cozy little cafe, the kind with dim lighting and warm, earthy tones. As they sipped their coffee, Ethan shared more about his past, the moments that had shaped him, the experiences that had left scars he still carried. Clara listened, absorbing each revelation, each painful detail, as if piecing together a puzzle.

"I've always been drawn to the shadows," he admitted, a hint of self-deprecation in his tone. "Maybe because it felt safer there, away from expectations, away from people who'd only see the broken parts of me."

Clara nodded, understanding more than she wanted to admit. She, too, had felt that pull—the comfort of solitude, the safety of silence. "I think we all have shadows," she said softly. "It's just a matter of how much we let them control us."

Ethan looked at her, his gaze intense, filled with something she hadn't seen before. "You make me want to be better, Clara. You make me want to face those shadows."

Her heart skipped a beat at his words, a warmth spreading through her. She knew she was still hurt, still guarded, but she couldn't deny the connection growing between them, a fragile bond built on honesty and vulnerability.

"Maybe we can help each other," she whispered, barely realizing she'd spoken aloud.

He reached across the table, his fingers brushing hers. "I'd like that."

As the weeks turned into months, their connection deepened. They spent hours talking, sharing memories, fears, and dreams they'd once kept hidden. Slowly, the walls Clara had built around her heart began to fall, and in their place, a new trust blossomed—a cautious, delicate trust that felt as fragile as glass.

But not everyone was happy about their newfound closeness.

One evening, Clara received a cryptic message on her phone. It was from an unknown number, the words cold and unsettling: "You don't know who you're dealing with. Walk away before it's too late."

Her heart pounded as she reread the message, a chill running down her spine. She tried to dismiss it as a prank, a meaningless threat, but deep down, she felt a lingering sense of unease.

When she told Ethan about it, his face hardened, his expression darkening with a mix of anger and fear. "Did you recognize the number?" he asked, his voice low.

Clara shook her head. "No. But it felt… personal, somehow."

Ethan clenched his fists, a look of grim determination in his eyes. "It's Daniel. He must've found out about us."

The realization hit her like a punch to the gut. Daniel, the man she thought she had left behind, the man she had tried so hard to forget, was back. And this time, he was determined to make his presence known.

"What does he want?" she whispered, fear tightening her throat.

Ethan looked at her, his gaze fierce. "He wants control. He's never been able to handle the idea of you being free of him. And now that he knows I'm in the picture, he'll do anything to break us apart."

In the days that followed, the messages continued, each one more threatening than the last. Daniel's words became increasingly sinister, laced with threats that left Clara feeling constantly on edge, her sense of safety slipping away with each passing day.

Ethan insisted on staying close to her, a protective presence that both reassured and terrified her. She knew he would do anything to keep her safe, but the lengths he was willing to go frightened her just as much as Daniel's threats.

One night, as they sat in her apartment, Ethan took her hand, his expression serious. "Clara, I need you to trust me on this. I have contacts, people who can help us. But you need to be honest with me about everything Daniel ever did to you, every threat he ever made."

She hesitated, memories of Daniel's cruelty rising to the surface, her heart heavy with the weight of the past. "He was controlling," she began, her voice barely a whisper. "Manipulative. There were times I felt like he saw right through me, like he knew every weakness I had and wasn't afraid to use it."

Ethan's grip on her hand tightened, his expression darkening. "He's not going to win this time, Clara. I won't let him."

But even as he spoke, a nagging fear crept into her mind. Ethan was willing to protect her, to stand by her side no matter the cost. But at what point did protection become possession? And at what cost would he be willing to stop Daniel?

As she looked into his eyes, she saw the fire there, the fierce determination that had once drawn her to him. But now, she wondered if that same fire would be the very thing that consumed them both.

The tension escalated, a dark cloud settling over their lives as Daniel's threats grew more menacing. Ethan's contacts tried to trace the messages, but Daniel was elusive, always one step ahead, his presence a haunting specter that shadowed their every move.

One night, Clara awoke to the sound of glass shattering. She bolted upright, her heart pounding, and saw Ethan already on his feet, his eyes fierce and alert.

"Stay here," he commanded, moving toward the door.

"Ethan, wait—" she whispered, fear gripping her, but he was already gone, disappearing into the darkness.

She waited, her pulse racing, every second stretching into an eternity. Finally, she heard footsteps approaching, and Ethan reappeared, his face tight with anger.

"It was him," he muttered, his jaw clenched. "He's getting bolder."

Clara felt a shiver run through her, the weight of their situation pressing down on her. "What does he want, Ethan? Why won't he leave us alone?"

Ethan looked at her, his eyes dark with a fury she had never seen before. "He wants to break you, Clara. He can't stand the idea of you being free of him, of you choosing me over him."

Her heart ached at the realization, the sense of helplessness overwhelming her. "How much longer can we live like this? Always looking over our shoulders, always afraid?"

Ethan's gaze softened, and he took her hands in his, his touch warm and steady. "Not much longer," he promised. "I'm going to put an end to this, Clara. Whatever it takes."

But as she looked into his eyes, she saw a darkness there that matched Daniel's, a willingness to do whatever was necessary. And in that moment, she realized that the man she loved might be just as dangerous as the one she feared.

Clara felt herself growing more isolated as the days wore on, the lines between protection and obsession blurring in ways that left her feeling trapped. Ethan's constant presence was both comforting and stifling, his determination to keep her safe bordering on possessive. She wondered if their relationship had become more about defying Daniel than about love.

One evening, as they sat in her dimly lit living room, Ethan reviewed the latest messages from Daniel. His jaw was clenched, his eyes fixed on the screen with a simmering rage. Clara reached out, placing a hand on his arm.

"Ethan," she murmured, trying to ground him, to pull him back to the moment. "Maybe... maybe there's another way. Maybe I could talk to him. Ask him what he really wants."

He looked at her sharply, his face a mask of disbelief. "Talk to him? Are you serious? Clara, he's a predator. He doesn't want to talk—he wants control. He'll manipulate you all over again."

She felt a flare of defiance rise within her, a desire to reclaim her agency, to face her own fears without hiding behind Ethan. "But this can't go on forever, Ethan. I need closure. I need to understand why he's doing this."

Ethan shook his head, his expression darkening. "You don't owe him anything. All he wants is to destroy you, to destroy us. I won't let him pull you back into his games."

Clara sighed, frustration bubbling beneath the surface. "But this isn't just about you protecting me, Ethan. It's about me taking control of my life. If I don't confront him, I'll always feel like he has power over me."

He softened slightly, his gaze shifting from anger to something more conflicted. "Clara, I... I just don't want to lose you," he admitted quietly. "If anything happened to you, I don't know what I'd do."

She looked into his eyes, seeing the vulnerability hidden behind his fierce protectiveness. She reached for his hand, squeezing it gently. "I know. But I need you to trust me too, Ethan. Let me handle this my way, just once."

THREE
CROSSING THE LINE

Ethan reluctantly agreed to give Clara space, but the tension between them remained, unspoken yet palpable. Clara could feel the weight of his worry pressing down on her, even as she tried to hold on to her own sense of agency.

The next morning, she received a message from Daniel. "Meet me at the old pier. Tonight at midnight. Come alone."

Her pulse quickened as she read the words, a mixture of fear and determination flooding her. She knew it was risky, that she was walking straight into his trap. But she also knew this was the confrontation she had been avoiding for too long.

When she told Ethan, his reaction was immediate. "No. Absolutely not. It's a trap, Clara, you can't go."

"I have to," she replied, her voice steady despite the fear gnawing at her. "This is the only way to end this."

Ethan's face twisted with anger and desperation. "You don't have to do this alone. Let me come with you."

She shook her head, steeling herself. "If you're there, he'll see it as a threat. I need him to think he has the upper hand."

Ethan's fists clenched, his face darkening with frustration. "This is exactly what he wants, Clara. He's using your need for closure against you."

"Maybe," she admitted. "But I can't keep living like this. I need to confront him, to understand why he's so obsessed. And if I don't face him now, I'll never be free."

He stared at her, his face a mixture of anger and fear, and then nodded reluctantly. "Fine. But I'm not letting you go completely unprotected." He pulled a small, sleek device from his pocket—a tracking device. "Keep this with you. I'll be close by, even if you can't see me."

Clara hesitated but finally agreed, tucking the device into her pocket. With a final, lingering glance at Ethan, she walked out of the apartment, her heart pounding as she prepared herself for the confrontation ahead.

As midnight approached, Clara found herself standing alone on the deserted pier, the cold night air biting against her skin. The water was calm, dark, stretching into the distance like an endless abyss. She wrapped her arms around herself, the quietness around her both comforting and eerie.

And then, she heard footsteps.

She turned to see Daniel emerging from the shadows, his face illuminated by the faint glow of a distant streetlight. He looked different than she remembered—older, wearier, but his eyes still held that familiar, predatory gleam.

"Clara," he greeted her, his voice smooth, almost cordial. "I knew you'd come."

Her heart pounded, but she kept her voice steady. "What do you want, Daniel? Why can't you leave me alone?"

He smiled, a cold, calculating expression. "Leave you alone? Clara, I thought we understood each other better than that. You and I, we have... unfinished business."

She shook her head, taking a step back. "Whatever connection we had is long gone, Daniel. I'm done with your games."

He chuckled, his gaze never leaving hers. "Oh, Clara. You really think you can just walk away? I know you, better than you know yourself. You thrive on the thrill, the danger. That's why you're here tonight."

A chill ran down her spine at his words, but she refused to let him see her fear. "You don't know me, Daniel. You never did. And

I'm not the same person you could control."

He tilted his head, studying her with an unsettling intensity. "Perhaps. But you're still drawn to the darkness, aren't you? That's why you found yourself tangled up with someone like Ethan."

The mention of Ethan jolted her, but she kept her expression neutral. "This isn't about him. This is about you and your need for control. I won't let you hold that power over me anymore."

Daniel's smile faded, this eyes hardening. "You think you have a choice, Clara? I always get what I want."

Before she could respond, Daniel stepped closer, his face twisted in a mixture of anger and obsession. "I let you go once, Clara, and look where it got us. You're here, drawn back to me like a moth to flame. You're mine, whether you want to admit it or not."

Clara forced herself to stand tall, meeting his gaze with defiance. "I'm not yours, Daniel. I never was. Whatever control you think you have is an illusion."

He sneered, his eyes narrowing. "Is it? Because from where I stand, you're alone, vulnerable. And Ethan—he's not the saint you think he is. How do you know he's not using you just as much as I did?"

Her chest tightened at his words, a flicker of doubt momentarily breaking through her resolve. But she pushed it down, refusing to let him poison her thoughts. "Whatever mistakes Ethan made, he's not you, Daniel. He doesn't feed off others' pain."

Daniel's gaze turned cold, and he took another step forward, closing the distance between them. "You're naïve, Clara. People don't change. You think Ethan is different? He's just another broken soul clinging to you because he can't face himself."

Her fingers clenched into fists, but she kept her voice steady. "Enough, Daniel. I came here to end this, to tell you that you have no power over me anymore. Whatever hold you had on me is gone."

He paused, his face unreadable. Then, in one swift movement, he grabbed her wrist, pulling her close. "You think you can walk away that easily?" he hissed, his grip tightening painfully. "I made you who you are. Without me, you're nothing."

Her heart raced, panic clawing at her as she struggled against his grip. But just as the fear threatened to overwhelm her, she heard footsteps approaching from behind.

"Let her go, Daniel."

The voice was calm, steady, yet filled with an underlying fury. She turned to see Ethan standing there, his eyes cold as he faced Daniel.

Daniel laughed, releasing her and stepping back, his gaze shifting between the two of them with twisted amusement. "Well, well. Isn't this touching? The hero comes to save the day."

Ethan's expression remained unreadable, his voice dangerously low. "This ends now, Daniel. Walk away, or you'll regret it."

Daniel smirked, but Clara saw a flicker of uncertainty in his eyes. He straightened, sneering as he looked at her one last time. "Fine. Have your fairy tale ending, Clara. But remember this—I'll always be a part of you."

With that, he turned and disappeared into the shadows, leaving her and Ethan standing alone on the empty pier.

As the silence settled, Clara felt her knees weaken, the adrenaline ebbing away to reveal a raw, vulnerable exhaustion. Ethan moved toward her, his gaze softening as he reached out to steady her.

"Are you okay?" he asked, his voice gentle, a stark contrast to the fierce protectiveness he had shown moments before.

She nodded, though her heart still hammered, a mixture of relief and lingering fear flooding her system. "I'm... I think so. I just... I needed to confront him. I needed to face him and make it clear that he doesn't control me anymore."

Ethan nodded, his expression softening as he looked at her with a mix of pride and worry. "You did. And you were stronger than he ever expected. I don't think he'll come after you again."

She took a shaky breath, feeling a weight lifting from her shoulders, though a faint unease still lingered. "I hope you're right. I can't keep living in fear. I just want peace, Ethan. I want to feel safe again."

He reached out, brushing a stray lock of hair from her face, his touch gentle. "You will be. I'll make sure of it."

Clara looked into his eyes, feeling a surge of gratitud

with something deeper, a connection that had only grown stronger through everything they'd endured. But even as she felt that warmth, a flicker of doubt gnawed at her. Could she really trust him completely? Or was there a part of him still shadowed in darkness?

But tonight, she was too tired to overthink, too drained to question. For now, she just wanted to feel the comfort of his presence, to let herself believe in the safety he promised. She leaned into him, allowing herself to let go, even if just for a moment.

"Take me home, Ethan," she whispered, her voice barely audible over the sound of the waves lapping against the pier.

He wrapped his arm around her, holding her close as they walked away from the shadows of the past, toward an uncertain, yet hopeful future.

The next morning, Clara woke with a strange sense of calm, as if a storm had finally passed. The encounter with Daniel felt like a nightmare, distant yet impactful, but she knew she had made the right choice in facing him. Still, the doubts about Ethan lingered, subtle but persistent, like a shadow she couldn't shake.

She spent the day in quiet reflection, trying to process everything that had happened, to make sense of the tumultuous journey that had brought her here. But as evening fell, she found herself yearning for the simplicity of her old life, the life before all the chaos.

Ethan arrived at her apartment that evening, bringing with him a bouquet of flowers, a small smile softening his otherwise intense features. "I thought you might want something beautiful after everything," he said, holding out the flowers.

Clara smiled, touched by the gesture. "Thank you, Ethan. I... I needed this."

They sat together, sharing a quiet dinner, the atmosphere between them both comforting and charged with unspoken words. Finally, as they finished their meal, Ethan looked at her, his gaze thoughtful.

"Clara," he began, his voice hesitant, "I know things have been... complicated. But I want you to know that I'm here for you, no matter what. I want us to have a fresh start, to move past everything that's happened."

She looked down, her fingers tracing patterns on the table. "I want that too, Ethan. But it's hard. There are still things I don't understand, things I'm afraid to even ask."

He reached for her hand, his grip reassuring. "Ask me anything. I don't want there to be secrets between us anymore."

She met his gaze, searching his eyes for any sign of deception. "Then tell me—why did you get involved with Daniel in the first place? What was it that tied you to him?"

Ethan's face darkened, his hand pulling away as he looked down, clearly grappling with his response.

After a long silence, he finally spoke, his voice barely above a whisper. "Daniel and I... we have a history. We were both drawn to the same world, a world that feeds on power, control, manipulation. But while he embraced it, I tried to escape."

Clara's heart sank as she listened, piecing together fragments of his past. "You mean... you were like him?"

Ethan shook his head, a pained look crossing his face. "Not like him. But I was willing to do things I'm not proud of. I thought I could use his methods to help people, to make a difference. But it was a lie. The truth is, I lost myself in that darkness, just as he did."

He looked up, his expression raw and vulnerable. "Meeting you changed that. You made me realize there was still a chance for me, that I didn't have to be like him. That's why I stayed away from you for so long, why I tried to keep my distance."

Clara's heart ached as she absorbed his confession. She could feel the conflict within him, the battle between the man he wanted to be and the darkness he couldn't fully leave behind. "But you still carry that with you, don't you? That part of you that's drawn to the darkness."

He nodded, his gaze steady. "I do. And I know it's a part of me that I'll always struggle with. But for you, I'll keep fighting it, Clara. I'll keep choosing the light."

She reached out, taking his hand in hers, a surge of emotion flooding through her. She knew there were no easy answers, no guarantees that they wouldn't face more challenges. But for now, she wanted to believe in him, in the man he was trying to become.

"Then let's take it one day at a time," she said softly, a small smile lifting the corners of her mouth. "Let's find a way to build something real, something free from all the shadows."

He smiled, relief evident in his eyes. "I'd like that."

And as they sat there, hands entwined, Clara felt a spark of hope flicker within her, a fragile light in the darkness they had both come to know so well.

Over the next few weeks, Clara and Ethan settled into a tentative routine, working to build a new life together, free from Daniel's shadow. Yet, the peace felt fragile, as if any moment, the past might come crashing back in.

One afternoon, Clara sat at a local café, sipping coffee and watching the world go by. She felt a strange blend of calm and anticipation, like she was waiting for something she couldn't name. Just as she began to relax, her phone vibrated on the table.

It was a message from an unknown number. Her heart raced as she opened it, her stomach twisting as she read the words: "You think you're safe, Clara? I'm still watching."

The message hit her like a punch to the gut, and she looked around the café, half-expecting to see Daniel's face among the strangers. But there was nothing, no sign of him, only the growing dread settling over her.

Her hands shook as she texted Ethan, her fingers clumsy as she typed. "I got a message from Daniel. He says he's still watching."

Within minutes, Ethan replied: "Stay there. I'm coming."

True to his word, he arrived shortly afterward, his face set in a grim expression as he scanned the café. He sat down across from her, his hand reaching out to steady hers.

"Are you okay?" he asked, his voice low and soothing.

Clara nodded, though her heart still raced. "I thought it was over, Ethan. I thought he'd given up."

Ethan's jaw tightened, his eyes darkening. "This is his way of keeping control, of making sure you never feel safe. But he's wrong. I'll find a way to stop him."

She looked down, the familiar weight of fear settling over her. "I don't know how much more I can take, Ethan. I just want this nightmare to end."

Ethan's hand tightened over hers, his gaze fierce. "It will end. I promise you, Clara. But we'll need to be smart, to stay one step ahead of him."

They left the café, and Ethan took her back to his apartment, where he had set up a few extra security measures to keep her safe. As they entered, Clara noticed the new locks, the small surveillance cameras he had installed near the doors and windows. It was a stark reminder of how much their lives had changed, of the ever-present threat hanging over them.

Ethan turned to her, his expression softening. "I know it feels like overkill, but I want you to feel safe here. This place—it's yours as much as mine."

She smiled weakly, touched by his dedication but weary of constantly looking over her shoulder. "Thank you, Ethan. I just wish... I wish I could go back to a time before all of this."

He nodded, a sympathetic look in his eyes. "We'll get there, Clara. But for now, I need you to trust me. Trust that I'll do whatever it takes to keep you safe."

She nodded, forcing herself to believe his words. But as the days passed, the unease only grew. She couldn't shake the feeling that Daniel was still watching, that he was waiting for the perfect moment to strike again. Every shadow, every sound outside the window made her jump, and sleep became elusive, her nights filled with restless dreams.

One evening, after another sleepless night, Clara decided she couldn't keep living in fear. She knew Ethan was doing everything he could to protect her, but she needed to feel a sense of control over her own life again.

"I want to do something, Ethan," she said as they sat together, the quiet hum of the city filtering through the apartment's walls. "I want to find a way to confront Daniel, to make sure he knows I'm not afraid of him anymore."

Ethan looked at her, concern etched across his face. "Confronting him could be exactly what he wants, Clara. He feeds off of this—the power, the fear."

"I know," she replied, her voice steady. "But I need to reclaim my own power. If I keep running, keep hiding, I'll never feel like myself again."

He studied her for a long moment, his gaze searching. Finally, he nodded. "Then we'll face him together. But we have to be careful, Clara. We can't let him manipulate us."

They began to make a plan, working together to gather evidence of Daniel's harassment, preparing themselves for the confrontation they both knew was inevitable. Clara felt a renewed sense of strength, as if she was finally reclaiming her life, bit by bit. But even as they strategized, a part of her knew that facing Daniel again would come at a cost, one she wasn't sure she was ready to pay.

Their plan took shape over the next few days. They gathered every message, every threat Daniel had sent, compiling a record that they could bring to the authorities if necessary. But as the deadline for confronting him drew near, Clara couldn't shake the feeling that they were walking straight into his trap.

The night before their planned meeting, she lay awake, her mind racing with thoughts of everything that had led her here. She felt Ethan's steady breathing beside her, his presence grounding her, giving her the strength she needed. Yet the fear lingered, a dark cloud that refused to dissipate.

She rose quietly, stepping out onto the balcony to take in the cool night air. The city stretched out below her, alive with lights and sounds, a reminder of the life she was fighting to protect.

Behind her, she heard Ethan's footsteps as he joined her on the balcony, his arm wrapping around her shoulders. "Couldn't sleep?"

She shook her head, leaning into his warmth. "I keep wondering if we're doing the right thing, if confronting him will only make things worse."

He tightened his hold on her, his voice gentle. "No matter what happens, we're in this together. You don't have to face him alone."

They stood in silence, watching the city lights flicker in the distance, both knowing that the confrontation with Daniel would change everything. For better or worse, they would finally face the shadows that had haunted them for so long.

FOUR

ALLIES AND ENEMIES

The day of the confrontation arrived, and Clara felt an uneasy determination settle over her. She and Ethan planned to meet Daniel in a public place, where they would feel some measure of safety. But as they prepared to leave, Ethan received an unexpected call. His face went pale as he listened to the person on the other end.

"Are you sure?" he asked, his voice tense. He looked at Clara, his expression unreadable as he ended the call. "There's something you need to know, Clara. Something I never told you."

Clara's stomach dropped, her mind racing. "What do you mean?"

Ethan took a deep breath, his gaze hardening. "There's a reason Daniel has been targeting you so obsessively. You're not just someone he picked to torment. He believes... he believes you're the key to something much bigger. Something that goes back to your past."

"My past?" Clara felt a chill run down her spine. "What are you talking about?"

"There's a part of your family history that's tied to Daniel's obsession with control and power. He thinks... he thinks you have access to something he desperately wants, something that could change everything."

Clara shook her head, bewildered. "That's impossible. My family—my parents were just ordinary people. There's nothing special about us."

Ethan's face darkened, a look of guilt flashing across his features. "There's more, Clara. Daniel's fixation on you—it's not just about power. It's personal. He believes your father knew a secret that could destroy him, something he never told you."

Clara's heart pounded as she tried to process Ethan's words. "But my father... he died when I was young. He was a quiet, gentle man. There's no way he was involved in anything dangerous."

"I know it sounds impossible, but Daniel's convinced that you inherited something, a key or a code, that your father left behind. And he won't stop until he has it."

Clara stared at Ethan, trying to make sense of the revelation. "Why didn't you tell me this before?"

Ethan looked away, his expression pained. "I thought I could keep you safe without dragging you into all of this. I didn't want you to feel like you were just a pawn in someone else's game. But now... now I realize you deserve to know the truth."

ey decided to confront Daniel in a secluded part of the city, a small park surrounded by towering trees. Clara felt the weight of her father's hidden past pressing down on her, filling her with both fear and a strange sense of curiosity. If there really was something her father had left for her, something that could end Daniel's reign of terror, she needed to know.

As they waited, Daniel appeared, his presence as chilling as ever, with a smirk that sent a cold shiver through Clara. He walked toward them slowly, his eyes never leaving hers.

"Ah, Clara. You finally decided to stop hiding," he sneered, his voice laced with mockery. "And you brought Ethan. How predictable."

Clara forced herself to stand tall, her voice steady. "I'm here to end this, Daniel. Whatever you think my father left me, it doesn't exist. You're chasing a ghost."

He laughed, a low, sinister sound. "Oh, Clara, your innocence is almost charming. But I know your father wasn't the man you thought he was. He had secrets—secrets he hid from you. And I'm going to make you remember."

Clara felt a knot of fear tighten in her stomach, but she refused to let him see her weakness. "You don't scare me, Daniel. Whatever power you think you have over me, it's over."

Daniel's smirk faded, replaced by a dark, unreadable expression. "We'll see about that," he said, pulling out an old, tattered envelope from his coat pocket and holding it up.

Clara's breath caught as she recognized her father's handwriting on the front of the envelope. "Where did you get that?"

"That's for me to know," he replied with a cold smile. "Inside this letter is the beginning of the truth, a truth your father hid from you. And if you want to know more, you'll have to play my game."

Clara reached for the envelope, her hands trembling, but Daniel pulled it back, taunting her. "Not so fast. You didn't think I'd just hand it over, did you?"

Ethan took a step forward, his voice low and threatening. "If you hurt her, I swear I'll—"

Daniel chuckled. "Spare me the heroics, Ethan. We both know you're in no position to make threats. You're as much a part of this as I am."

Ethan clenched his fists, but Daniel held his gaze, unfazed. "Remember, Clara, your father's secrets aren't just his own. They're tied to both of us—whether you like it or not."

Clara's voice was barely a whisper as she asked, "What do you mean?"

Daniel's smile widened. "Let's just say, your father and I had unfinished business. He left you clues—clues that will lead you to the truth. But it's up to you if you want to uncover it."

She looked at him, struggling to suppress her fear. "What kind of game are you playing?"

"The kind that will force you to choose, Clara. You can walk away and live a simple life... or you can find out the truth and risk everything. But I assure you, once you open that envelope, there's no going back."

Clara stared at the envelope, her pulse racing. A part of her wanted to throw it away, to reject whatever secrets it held. But another part of her—the part that needed closure—demanded answers. She took a deep breath and nodded.

Daniel handed over the envelope with a smirk. "Good girl. But remember, Clara, once you're in, you're in for life. I'll be watching."

With that, he turned and disappeared into the shadows, leaving Clara and Ethan standing alone, the envelope heavy in her hands. She could feel the weight of it, the mystery of her father's past now a tangible presence in her life.

Ethan placed a hand on her shoulder. "Are you sure you want to do this?"

Clara met his gaze, her expression resolute. "I need to know, Ethan. Whatever my father was hiding, it's time I found out."

They went back to Ethan's apartment, where Clara opened the envelope with trembling hands. Inside, she found a single photograph and a letter, both worn and faded with age. The photograph showed her father standing beside a man who looked disturbingly familiar.

She glanced at Ethan, her voice barely a whisper. "This man... it's Daniel."

Ethan looked shocked. "But that's impossible. This picture has to be at least twenty years old."

Clara read the letter, her father's words filling her with both dread and determination. He warned her of a secret society that Daniel was part of, one that sought power through manipulation and control, one he had once been close to but left behind. He urged her to stay hidden, to live a simple life and avoid Daniel at all costs.

But there was also a cryptic message at the end: "The past cannot be erased, Clara. You must find the Key of Unity and end what I could not."

She looked at Ethan, the weight of her father's secret now shared between them. "We have to find this key, Ethan. Whatever my father couldn't finish… we have to end it."

Ethan nodded, his expression fierce. "Then we'll face this together. We'll end Daniel's game once and for all."

The following days were a blur of research and dead ends as Clara and Ethan tried to decipher her father's cryptic letter. They poured over old family records, visited places from Clara's childhood, and even tried contacting people her father had known, hoping someone could shed light on the mysterious "Key of Unity."

But every path they followed seemed to lead to a dead end, as if her father's life had been meticulously erased. It wasn't until Clara remembered a dusty, forgotten box her mother had kept in the attic that they stumbled upon their first real clue.

The box contained her father's old journals, each page filled with his precise handwriting. As Clara flipped through the yellowed pages, she came across an entry dated the night before he died. In it, he wrote about the Key of Unity, mentioning a symbol—a circle with an inverted triangle inside—drawn hastily in the margin.

She showed the drawing to Ethan, who frowned. "I've seen this symbol before. It's linked to an old, secretive group called The Ascendants. They were rumored to have been around for centuries, controlling people from the shadows. If Daniel is part of this group, it would explain a lot."

Clara's mind raced. "But why would my father be connected to them? He was just a schoolteacher. He never spoke about anything dangerous or secretive."

"Maybe he was trying to protect you," Ethan suggested. "Or maybe he was deeper into this world than you knew."

They decided to dig deeper into The Ascendants, scouring libraries, archives, and hidden corners of the internet. But information was scarce. Any record of the group was veiled in legend and conspiracy, with nothing concrete to guide them.

Then, one evening, while browsing an old forum on secret societies, Ethan found a post from someone claiming to have left The Ascendants and warning others of its dangers. The user's screen name was "LostSoul17," and their last post was nearly a decade old, but it mentioned something startling: "The Key of Unity is not just a thing—it's an idea, a power that can only be unlocked by those who know true unity, beyond fear."

Clara felt a chill run through her. "True unity? What could that mean?"

Ethan thought for a moment. "It sounds like it's not just an object but a mindset, something Daniel has been after for power, but that only someone with pure intentions can access."

Clara frowned, a realization dawning on her. "My father must have believed I could access it, that somehow I held the key. That's why he left that letter, why he warned me."

But before they could make sense of it, Ethan's phone vibrated. It was another message—from Daniel.

"Impressive work. You're getting close. But remember, every step brings you closer to me. Are you ready to face the truth?"

The message made her blood run cold. Daniel was still watching, still waiting, and she realized that this chase wasn't just about discovering her father's secret—it was a battle for her own strength and resolve.

They decided to take a different approach, heading to an abandoned estate on the outskirts of town that her father had once taken her to as a child. It had been a place of peace, somewhere he went for solitude. Now, she wondered if it was a place he went to hide.

As they wandered through the old rooms, Clara spotted a worn, leather-bound book tucked away in a dusty shelf. Inside was a single, strange note:

"When the one with the strongest will faces their own darkness, only then can the Key reveal itself."

Clara felt a shiver of understanding. Her father had hidden these clues for her, knowing that someday she would face Daniel, that she would need to summon a strength she didn't yet understand.

Ethan glanced over her shoulder. "Clara, this isn't just about finding a physical key. It's about you confronting something within yourself, maybe something that Daniel believes will unlock this 'unity' he's obsessed with."

She looked up, feeling the weight of her father's message settle over her. "I think I know what he meant. My father believed that strength lies in facing our darkest fears without letting them control us. Maybe he meant that to access this 'Key,' I'd need to face my deepest fears... and overcome them."

Ethan nodded, understanding dawning in his eyes. "Daniel is counting on you to give in to fear. But if you can stand up to him without it... maybe that's the real key."

As they pieced together her father's clues, Clara felt a strange calm settle over her. She realized that this was her father's legacy—a way to protect her, to empower her to break free from Daniel's influence. All she had to do now was confront him, once and for all.

They set up a meeting in the same park, but this time, Clara wasn't filled with dread. Instead, she felt a fierce determination growing within her.

When Daniel arrived, he wore his usual smug expression, but Clara didn't flinch. She met his gaze with a newfound strength, refusing to let fear show.

"I know what you want," she said, her voice steady. "And I'm here to tell you that you'll never have it."

Daniel's eyes narrowed, his calm facade slipping. "Do you think you can just walk away from this? Your father may have tried to keep you from the truth, but you're in deeper than you realize."

Clara took a deep breath, channeling every ounce of courage she had. "The truth is, you don't have power over me. You never did. The real power isn't in secrets or threats—it's in facing the darkness and not letting it define us."

For a moment, Daniel seemed taken aback, as if her words had pierced through his cold exterior. But then his face twisted into a sneer. "Nice speech, but words won't protect you. You'll fall, just like your father did."

But as he reached for her, something unexpected happened. Clara felt a surge of warmth within her, a sense of unity and clarity that seemed to radiate outward. It was as if her father's words were finally manifesting, a strength that protected her, rendering Daniel's threats powerless.

Daniel's sneer faded, replaced by a look of confusion and fear. He stumbled back, his control over her shattered by the realization that she was no longer his to manipulate.

Ethan stepped forward, his expression triumphant. "It's over, Daniel. You lost the moment Clara stopped fearing you."

Daniel's face contorted with rage, but he said nothing. He turned and walked away, disappearing into the shadows, defeated by a force he couldn't understand.

Clara felt a sense of release, as if a weight had been lifted from her soul. Her father's message had been clear: true unity wasn't a key or an object—it was a power that came from within, from overcoming fear and reclaiming her life.

She turned to Ethan, her heart pounding with relief and newfound strength. "It's finally over, isn't it?"

Ethan smiled, his eyes full of pride. "Yes, Clara. You did it. You beat him."

They embraced, standing together in the quiet of the night, both knowing that they had emerged from the darkness stronger than ever.

Clara held the faded photograph in her trembling hands, the hidden figure casting a shadow over the image. Her father had been part of something bigger, something dangerous. And whoever had sent her the key wanted her to follow in his footsteps, to unravel secrets he had kept hidden for so long.

Ethan placed a reassuring hand on her shoulder. "Clara, we don't have to do this. We could walk away, leave the past behind."

But Clara shook her head, a fire igniting in her chest. "No. My father was protecting something—maybe protecting me. If he left clues, he must have wanted me to find them. I need to know the truth."

They carefully packed up the photograph and the note, taking the small key with them. On the drive back, Clara's mind raced with questions. Who were the people in the photograph? And why had her father kept them a secret from her?

That night, as they sat at Ethan's kitchen table, Clara laid out all the clues they had gathered so far. The old journals, the cryptic symbols, the letter warning her of The Ascendants—all pieces of a puzzle that seemed impossible to solve.

Ethan studied the photograph again, his brow furrowing. "The room they're in... it looks like some kind of underground chamber. Do you recognize it?"

Clara shook her head. "No, but it feels... familiar, somehow. Like I've seen it before, maybe in a dream."

Ethan's gaze softened. "It could be a memory, something from when you were young."

Clara's eyes widened as a memory flickered to life, hazy but unmistakable. "There was a basement in the old house we lived in before my father died. He used to keep it locked, and he always told me never to go down there."

Ethan nodded, sensing where she was going. "Do you think whatever he was hiding is still there?"

Clara clenched her fists, her pulse quickening. "There's only one way to find out."

FIVE

THE DEPTHS OF ECLIPSE

They made their way to Clara's childhood home the next day, hoping that it hadn't changed too much since her family had left. When they arrived, she felt a pang of nostalgia mixed with apprehension. The house looked almost exactly as she remembered it, with ivy creeping up the walls and the old oak tree swaying in the front yard.

The current owners were away for the weekend, so Ethan managed to slip them inside without raising any alarms. Clara led him down a narrow staircase to the basement door, which was still locked. With a bit of effort, Ethan managed to pry the door open, and they stepped inside.

The basement was cold and dark, with a musty smell that made Clara shiver. She fumbled for a light switch, and a dim bulb flickered to life, casting eerie shadows across the room. Dust covered every surface, and cobwebs hung from the ceiling like veils.

At the far end of the room, Clara spotted an old wooden trunk with her father's initials carved into the lid. She knelt beside it, her hands shaking as she lifted the lid. Inside, she found a collection of papers, each one filled with her father's handwriting. Maps, letters, symbols—an entire history she had never known about.

As she sifted through the papers, something caught her eye: a worn notebook with the symbol of The Ascendants on the cover.

She opened it, and a single phrase was scrawled across the first page:

"The Key of Unity is within you. Only by facing your own darkness can you unlock its power."

Ethan read over her shoulder, his face solemn. "It's like your father knew you'd end up here, searching for answers."

Clara nodded, a lump forming in her throat. "He must have been preparing me, even if I didn't realize it. He wanted me to find this."

Among the papers, Clara found a letter addressed to her. The ink was faded, but the words were clear:

"Clara, if you're reading this, it means you've taken the first step toward discovering the truth. The Ascendants will stop at nothing to gain power, and they believe you hold the key to that power. But remember, true strength doesn't come from control—it comes from unity, from facing the shadows within. Follow the path I've laid out for you, but trust no one. There are more secrets in our family than you can imagine. Stay strong, my daughter."

She felt tears prickling at the corners of her eyes. Her father had known the dangers, and he had left this trail of clues, trusting her to piece them together.

Ethan placed a comforting hand on her shoulder. "Your father believed in you, Clara. He believed you had the strength to finish what he couldn't."

Clara nodded, her resolve hardening. "I'm going to make sure his sacrifices weren't in vain. Whatever the Ascendants are planning, I'll stop them."

As they prepared to leave, Clara tucked the notebook and the letter into her bag. She glanced around the basement one last time, feeling her father's presence lingering in the shadows. This journey had taken her deeper than she ever could have imagined, but she was determined to see it through to the end.

Outside, the sun was beginning to set, casting long shadows across the yard. But Clara felt a sense of peace, a quiet confidence that she hadn't felt before. She knew that she was no longer the frightened, uncertain woman she had once been.

She was ready to face whatever darkness lay ahead. And with Ethan by her side, she knew she wasn't alone.

As they drove away from her childhood home, a new sense of purpose filled her heart. She had uncovered the first of her father's secrets, but she knew there were more answers waiting, hidden in the depths of a legacy she was only beginning to understand.

And for the first time, Clara felt certain that she would uncover the truth—no matter the cost.

In the days that followed, Clara became consumed by her father's legacy. Each clue and cryptic message unraveled more layers of a mystery that felt impossibly vast, as if her father's life had been an intricate puzzle crafted just for her.

She and Ethan spent hours poring over the notebook, deciphering passages that described The Ascendants' objectives and rituals. It was clear they were after more than just power; they sought influence over people's minds, a kind of control that went beyond manipulation. The "Key of Unity," as Clara's father had hinted, was somehow tied to resisting that power and unraveling their grip on others.

One passage in particular caught her attention:

"The mind is fragile, but it is also the strongest weapon we have. They want control over minds that cannot see their own darkness. But a mind that faces itself becomes invincible."

Ethan looked at her thoughtfully after reading the passage aloud. "It sounds like your father believed the Key of Unity isn't a physical thing—it's about self-awareness, about facing your own inner darkness."

Clara nodded, her gaze distant. "It makes sense. My father was always teaching me to confront my fears, even as a kid. Maybe he knew that the only way to be free of The Ascendants was to be unafraid of whatever darkness they tried to impose on us."

Ethan gave her a solemn nod. "So if we're going to fight them, we need to prepare ourselves mentally, too."

That evening, Clara went home to reflect on the darkness within her own life. She knew she couldn't move forward without confronting the parts of herself she had tried to bury. Memories surfaced: her father's sudden disappearance, the sense of abandonment she'd struggled with, and the fear that somehow, she might end up like him—consumed by secrets, cut off from the ones she loved.

She closed her eyes, letting the painful memories wash over her, resisting the urge to push them away. She could feel the weight lifting, the fear dissipating, as she acknowledged those parts of herself with compassion instead of shame.

The next morning, Clara felt a new strength within her. She met Ethan, who noticed the shift immediately.

"You seem different today," he said, smiling.

"I think I'm starting to understand," she replied, her voice calm. "I'm not afraid of what happened in the past anymore. I'm ready to face it, to face everything."

Ethan took her hand, squeezing it gently. "Then let's take the next step. Together."

Their next destination was a secluded cabin nestled in the woods, a location mentioned briefly in her father's notebook. It had been a meeting place for the original members of The Ascendants, where they held secret gatherings and exchanged information. Clara hoped it might hold answers—maybe even reveal the identities of the people in the photograph.

They arrived at the cabin under cover of night. The air was thick with tension as they approached the door, each step echoing in the stillness of the woods. Inside, the cabin was dimly lit by a single candle, its glow casting shadows across the room. Papers and old documents were scattered on a large table, abandoned by whoever had been here last.

Clara carefully sifted through the papers, her fingers brushing over faded handwriting and yellowed pages. Suddenly, she found a note addressed to her father:

"Daniel, we've come too far to stop now. The Key of Unity is within reach, but only if we hold our ground. You know what must be done."

Ethan glanced over her shoulder, reading the note. "Daniel? Isn't that the same man who threatened you?"

Clara's heart pounded. "Yes. He must have known my father... They must have worked together before something tore them apart."

She pieced together the fragments in her mind: her father and Daniel had once been allies, partners in some mysterious plan. But something must have changed, a betrayal or a disagreement that drove them apart and left her father fearing for his life—and hers.

As Clara and Ethan continued searching the cabin, they uncovered more clues that hinted at a split within The Ascendants, a power struggle that had turned deadly. One document detailed an argument over the "Key of Unity," suggesting that while some members saw it as a source of control, others viewed it as a way to liberate minds and souls.

Ethan looked at Clara, a realization dawning in his eyes. "Your father must have been one of the dissenters. He wanted the Key to be used for good, while Daniel saw it as a tool for domination."

Clara's mind raced, the pieces falling into place. "My father knew the dangers, but he believed in the Key's true purpose. That's why he hid everything from me, to protect me from Daniel and the others who would use it to hurt people."

As she spoke, her phone buzzed with a message. She glanced down, her heart skipping a beat when she saw it was from an unknown number.

"You're closer than you think, Clara. But be warned: the truth will destroy you."

Her hands trembled, and she showed the message to Ethan. "It's him. Daniel."

Ethan's expression hardened. "He's watching us. But that means he's also afraid of what we might find."

Clara steeled herself, her resolve unshakable. "Then we're on the right path. If Daniel is afraid of the truth, it's because he knows it's something he can't control."

With renewed determination, Clara and Ethan left the cabin, knowing that they were inching closer to the heart of the mystery. But with each step forward, they also knew that danger was closing in. Daniel was growing desperate, and desperate men were unpredictable.

The next day, they received an anonymous tip about an old library archive rumored to house information on secret societies and their rituals. The library, known for its vast collection of forbidden texts, held documents that few people even knew existed.

They arrived late in the evening, slipping into the archives after hours with the help of a friend of Ethan's who worked there. The place had an eerie quietness, the rows of ancient books towering over them as they searched for anything related to The Ascendants.

After hours of combing through dusty shelves, Clara found a tome filled with symbols and references to the "Unity of Minds." Her fingers traced the pages, and a chill ran down her spine when she saw an entry with her father's name listed among others—each one marked as "missing" or "deceased."

She swallowed hard, the weight of the revelation sinking in. "My father wasn't just hiding from Daniel; he was hiding from all of them."

Ethan nodded grimly. "And if Daniel knows we're getting this close, he won't stop until he silences us, too."

Clara looked at Ethan, a mixture of fear and determination in her gaze. "Then we have to stay ahead of him. Whatever it takes, we can't let them erase us like they did my father."

They exchanged a resolute glance, knowing that the deeper they ventured, the higher the stakes became. There was no turning back now.

The realization that Daniel and the other members of The Ascendants were actively monitoring their every move weighed heavily on Clara and Ethan as they left the library. Each footstep echoed in the dimly lit hallway, and Clara felt as though unseen eyes were following them, lurking in the shadows.

They returned to Ethan's apartment in silence, both lost in thought. The discovery of her father's name in the library's archive had confirmed her worst fears—her father's involvement with The Ascendants ran far deeper than she'd ever imagined.

As they entered the apartment, Ethan locked the door behind them and drew the blinds. "We need a plan, Clara. They're not going to stop until they get what they want, and they won't hesitate to go through us to do it."

Clara nodded, determination hardening her features. "We need to go on the offensive. If Daniel wants to play mind games, we'll beat him at his own game."

Ethan raised an eyebrow. "You're thinking we turn the tables?"

Clara's lips curved into a steely smile. "Exactly. They think they know everything about us, but maybe it's time we give them a few surprises of our own."

Over the next few days, Clara and Ethan put their plan into action. They knew they couldn't face The Ascendants directly—not yet. But they could disrupt their operations, expose their secrets bit by bit, and force Daniel to react.

They started by tracing the connections between her father's old associates, mapping out every name, every link, every possible weak point. Clara was relentless, combing through her father's journals, cross-referencing names with any public records they could find.

One night, she discovered a name that stood out: Dr. Evelyn Hart, a respected psychiatrist who had been part of The Ascendants but had left under mysterious circumstances. Her name appeared frequently in her father's notes, with mentions of "The Experiment" and "Mind Fragmentation."

Ethan read over her shoulder. "Think she'd talk to us?"

Clara looked up, a fire in her eyes. "She might, if we can convince her we're on her side. If she left The Ascendants, she must have had her reasons. And if she knows about 'Mind Fragmentation,' then she might be able to tell us what they're really after."

With a plan in place, Clara made contact with Dr. Hart, arranging a meeting in a remote coffee shop on the outskirts of town. They were taking a risk, but they both knew they needed answers.

The coffee shop was nearly empty when they arrived. Dr. Hart was already seated in a secluded corner, her eyes sharp and cautious as she watched them approach. She was older than Clara had expected, with streaks of silver in her hair and an aura of quiet intelligence.

"Dr. Hart?" Clara asked as she took a seat across from her.

Dr. Hart nodded, her gaze unwavering. "You must be Clara. You look just like your father."

Clara's breath caught. "You knew him well?"

Dr. Hart gave a sad smile. "Better than he probably wanted. We were both caught up in the same ideals... until he saw what The Ascendants were truly capable of. That's when he tried to protect you."

Clara leaned forward, urgency in her voice. "Please, tell us everything. What is 'Mind Fragmentation,' and why is Daniel after it?"

Dr. Hart hesitated, glancing around to make sure no one was listening. She took a deep breath. "Mind Fragmentation is a technique The Ascendants developed to control people, to break down the barriers of the conscious mind and implant suggestions directly. It's a form of mind control, Clara—a dark, insidious power that can manipulate people from the inside."

Ethan frowned, his voice low. "And the Key of Unity? How does that fit into all this?"

Dr. Hart's eyes flickered with fear. "The Key of Unity is the only known way to reverse the effects of Mind Fragmentation. It's a powerful mental resilience that protects someone from being controlled. Your father was one of the few who understood it, who embodied it. That's why they're so desperate to find it—they want to destroy anyone who possesses it."

Clara's heart pounded as the implications sank in. "So they think I might have this... Key of Unity?"

Dr. Hart nodded. "If Daniel believes you've inherited your father's strength, he'll stop at nothing to break you. You're a threat to everything they're building."

SIX

THE UNSEEN WAR

The weight of Dr. Hart's words settled over Clara like a storm cloud. She now understood why her father had kept his life with The Ascendants a secret, why he'd gone to such lengths to protect her. He hadn't just been hiding her—he'd been preparing her, hoping she'd have the strength to resist their influence.

Ethan looked at Dr. Hart, his jaw set. "How do we stop them?"

Dr. Hart glanced down, her fingers tracing the edge of her coffee cup. "There's a ceremony they're planning, one that involves everyone affected by Mind Fragmentation. It's their final step in solidifying control over their followers. If we can disrupt the ceremony, expose what they're doing, we might be able to break their influence for good."

Clara's mind raced. "Where is this ceremony taking place?"

Dr. Hart hesitated, her gaze troubled. "I don't know for sure. They're very secretive. But if you dig deep enough, you might find clues. Just be careful—Daniel is ruthless. He won't hesitate to hurt you if he feels threatened."

Clara met Dr. Hart's gaze, her own filled with a quiet resolve. "Thank you. For telling us the truth. My father would want us to finish what he started."

Dr. Hart offered a small nod, her expression one of weary understanding. "I hope you succeed, Clara. There's more at stake here than you realize."

After leaving the coffee shop, Clara and Ethan went straight back to his apartment to regroup. Armed with the knowledge Dr. Hart had given them, they felt both a renewed sense of purpose and a simmering fear of what lay ahead.

As they reviewed everything they'd gathered so far, Clara's phone buzzed again, the now-familiar sensation of dread tightening in her chest. It was another text from the unknown number.

"You can't stop us, Clara. We see everything. The Key will be ours."

Clara clenched her fists, anger flaring in her chest. She showed the message to Ethan, her voice steady. "They know we're getting close. But they're underestimating us."

Ethan gave her a determined nod. "We'll make them regret it."

With a deep breath, Clara began to plan their next move. They would start by searching for any mentions of locations linked to The Ascendants, hoping to find a lead on where the ceremony might be held. Time was running out, and every second brought them closer to a confrontation that would test them in ways they couldn't yet imagine.

But Clara was ready. She could feel the strength her father had instilled in her, a quiet resilience she had only just begun to understand. She wasn't just fighting for herself—she was fighting for the truth, for her father's memory, and for the freedom of everyone The Ascendants sought to control.

And she knew, deep down, that no matter how dark the path became, she would see it through to the end.

Clara's pulse quickened as she and Ethan poured over maps and documents, looking for any pattern that could reveal the location of The Ascendants' ceremony. The tension in the air was palpable, and each clue they uncovered seemed to pull them deeper into a shadowy web spun by powerful forces intent on keeping them in the dark.

Late that night, they stumbled upon a hidden page in her father's journal—a faded map, with a barely visible mark in the center. The location was a deserted estate on the outskirts of town, rumored to have been abandoned years ago under mysterious circumstances. Next to it, in her father's handwriting, were the words: "The Hollowed Ground. Where minds are lost and souls bound."

Ethan stared at the page, his brow furrowing. "The Hollowed Ground... sounds like something out of a nightmare. Do you think that's where they're holding the ceremony?"

Clara nodded slowly. "It has to be. This place—it's where they conducted their original experiments. My father must have visited it, seen what they were doing. And if he left us this clue, he wanted us to go there."

Ethan's face tightened. "Then we go in prepared. No surprises."

But Clara couldn't shake the ominous feeling twisting in her gut. Her father had left this note for her to find—but would she be walking straight into a trap?

The following night, Clara and Ethan drove out to the estate under cover of darkness. The road was winding and narrow, flanked by trees that seemed to close in around them like silent sentinels guarding a forbidden secret. As they approached, a dense fog rolled in, blanketing the estate grounds and giving the scene an eerie, ghostly feel.

The mansion loomed ahead, a hulking structure of crumbling stone and ivy-covered walls. It looked more like a ruin than a place of ritual, but Clara knew appearances could be deceiving.

They parked a safe distance away, approaching on foot to avoid detection. Clara's heart pounded as they reached the mansion's main doors, the oppressive silence settling over them. She glanced at Ethan, who nodded, his face set in grim determination.

Pushing open the heavy doors, they slipped inside, and the stale air wrapped around them like a suffocating shroud. The interior was dark, the only light coming from the occasional flicker of candles scattered throughout the rooms.

As they moved through the mansion, eerie whispers seemed to echo off the walls, growing louder with each step. Clara's skin prickled as she realized the whispers weren't random—they were chanting. A low, ominous hum that reverberated in her bones.

Ethan shot her a worried glance. "Do you hear that?"

Clara nodded, her face pale. "They're already here."

They crept down a narrow hallway that led deeper into the estate, following the sound of the chanting. Finally, they reached a massive, iron-bound door, slightly ajar. Clara peered inside, her heart hammering as she took in the scene before her.

In the center of the room, members of The Ascendants stood in a circle, clad in dark robes, their faces obscured. At the center of the circle was a small stone altar, covered with strange symbols and burning candles. But what sent a chill through Clara was the sight of Daniel, standing at the head of the group, his eyes cold and calculating as he surveyed the room.

In his hands, he held a small vial filled with a shimmering, dark liquid. He raised it high, his voice rising above the chanting. "Tonight, we rid ourselves of all obstacles. Tonight, we bind the final Key and claim true power!"

Ethan's hand gripped Clara's arm tightly, his voice a hoarse whisper. "That vial... what's he going to do with it?"

Clara swallowed hard, a sinking dread filling her. "He's going to use it to break the Key of Unity—whatever's left of it in their minds. He's planning to sever any trace of free will in these people."

They watched in horror as Daniel approached a young woman standing at the edge of the circle, her expression vacant, her eyes glassy as though she were trapped in some internal nightmare. Clara's chest tightened—this was more than mind control. It was as if these people were being stripped of their very souls.

Unable to stand by any longer, Clara stepped forward, her voice cutting through the chanting. "Daniel! Stop!"

The chanting ceased instantly as every head turned toward her. Daniel's expression shifted from surprise to amusement, his lips curving into a mocking smile. "Ah, Clara. I knew you'd come. You're more like your father than you realize."

Clara held her ground, her voice steady. "This ends tonight, Daniel. Whatever hold you have over these people, it dies here."

Daniel chuckled, taking a step closer. "You have no idea what you're up against, do you? Your father thought he could fight us, too, but he was weak. He didn't understand true power."

Clara's jaw clenched. "My father was stronger than you'll ever be. He understood that real strength doesn't come from control—it comes from freedom."

Daniel's eyes narrowed, a flicker of anger breaking through his calm demeanor. He lifted the vial, holding it between them like a weapon. "You think you're brave, standing here? I could end you with a single drop of this. Just like I did with your father."

The words hit her like a physical blow, and she felt her blood run cold. Her father hadn't simply disappeared—Daniel had killed him. She struggled to keep her composure, anger and grief warring within her.

"Then do it," she said, her voice barely a whisper. "If you think you're so powerful, prove it."

Daniel hesitated, clearly not expecting her challenge. His hand trembled slightly, and for the first time, Clara saw a crack in his confidence. But then, just as quickly, his expression hardened.

"Fine," he sneered. "I'll show you just how powerless you really are."

He uncorked the vial and moved toward her, his eyes filled with a dark intent. Clara steeled herself, ready for whatever horror he was about to unleash.

But before he could reach her, Ethan lunged forward, knocking the vial out of Daniel's hand. It shattered on the floor, the dark liquid spilling out and soaking into the stone, hissing as if alive.

Daniel screamed, fury twisting his features as he lunged at Ethan. "You fool! Do you have any idea what you've done?"

Ethan shoved him back, his voice a fierce snarl. "You're done, Daniel. This ends now."

With the vial destroyed, the atmosphere in the room changed. The other members of The Ascendants began to stir, as if waking from a deep sleep, confusion clouding their faces. Whatever spell Daniel had cast over them was broken.

Clara seized the opportunity, raising her voice above the chaos. "Everyone, listen to me! You're free now—you don't have to obey him anymore!"

A ripple of recognition passed through the group, and a few of them began backing away from Daniel, shaking off the remnants of his control. Panic flashed across his face as he realized he was losing his hold over them.

Desperate, he tried to rally them. "Don't listen to her! I am your leader—I hold the power of the Key! Without me, you are nothing!"

But his words fell on deaf ears. The crowd was turning against him, and for the first time, Daniel looked truly afraid.

Clara took a step closer to him, her voice filled with quiet fury. "It's over, Daniel. Whatever twisted control you had, it's gone. You have nothing left."

Daniel's face contorted with rage. He lunged toward her, his hands reaching for her throat, but Clara was ready. She sidestepped him, grabbing his arm and twisting it behind his back, immobilizing him with a strength she hadn't realized she possessed.

Ethan stepped forward, his gaze cold. "Leave. And if you ever come near Clara or anyone else again, you'll regret it."

For a moment, Daniel seemed ready to fight, but then his shoulders slumped in defeat. He wrenched himself out of Clara's grip and staggered toward the exit, his expression twisted with hatred and humiliation.

As he disappeared into the darkness, Clara felt a strange sense of release—a weight lifting off her shoulders. She had faced her darkest fears and won, but more importantly, she had honored her father's legacy.

Ethan placed a hand on her shoulder, his voice soft. "It's over, Clara. You're free."

Clara took a deep breath, feeling a sense of peace settle over her for the first time in years. She had finally broken the chains of The Ascendants, not just for herself, but for all the lives they had tried to control.

And in the silence that followed, she knew that her father was finally at peace too.

In the weeks that followed, life seemed to settle back into some semblance of normalcy for Clara and Ethan. The dark weight of The Ascendants had finally lifted, and the people who had once been controlled by Daniel's influence were beginning to reclaim their lives, free from manipulation.

Clara spent her days sorting through the remnants of her father's belongings, finding comfort in his journals and letters. She could finally read them without the sting of unanswered questions, knowing he had fought to protect her until his last breath. His sacrifice had freed not only her but countless others.

Ethan often joined her in this quiet work, their companionship deepening with each passing day. He was the steady presence she needed, a reminder that she wasn't alone. They had survived something horrific together, and that bond ran deeper than either of them could put into words.

One day, as they sorted through her father's papers, Ethan came across a small, locked box. He glanced at Clara, holding it up. "Do you know what's in here?"

Clara shook her head, taking the box from him. It was plain, wooden, and unmarked, but it felt heavy with significance. As she turned it over in her hands, she noticed a small, faint symbol carved into the bottom—a symbol she recognized from her father's journals as the mark of the Key of Unity.

She found a key among her father's things and unlocked the box, revealing a stack of papers and a single, worn photograph. The photo was of her father, smiling broadly, with a woman and a young child she recognized as herself. A wave of emotions washed over her as she held the photo, feeling a connection to a past she had nearly lost.

Beneath the photo, a letter lay folded. She opened it carefully, her heart racing as she read the familiar handwriting.

My Dearest Clara,

If you're reading this, then I am gone, and you are braver than I ever imagined. I kept secrets from you, not out of mistrust, but out of love. The Ascendants were a darkness that haunted me, and I couldn't allow them to reach you. I am sorry for what you've had to face because of my choices. But I know you are strong, Clara, and that you have the resilience to walk your own path.

Inside this box are my notes on the Key of Unity—what it truly means and why it's so important. You are the embodiment of that Key, Clara, the strength I never had. Carry this knowledge forward, and remember that the true power of the Key lies in freedom, in the ability to choose and to protect the ones we love.

Love always, Dad.

The words hit her like a tidal wave, filling her with a mixture of sorrow, pride, and resolution. Her father had known all along that she would need to carry on his fight, that she would be the one to finally put an end to The Ascendants' influence.

Ethan placed a comforting hand on her shoulder, and she leaned into him, allowing herself a moment of quiet peace.

SEVEN
BREAKING THE CHAINS

A few weeks later, Clara received an unexpected call. It was Dr. Hart, her voice calm but laced with urgency.

"Clara, I've uncovered something," she said. "Daniel may be gone, but some remnants of The Ascendants are still active. They're scattered, but they're trying to regroup. You may have broken their leader, but they're looking for a new way to regain control."

Clara felt a familiar chill at Dr. Hart's words. She had hoped it was over, that Daniel's defeat had been the end of it. But the scars left by The Ascendants ran deep, and their influence wasn't so easily erased.

"What do they want now?" Clara asked, her voice steady.

"They're searching for what they call 'the successor'—someone who can wield the Key of Unity's power. They believe it will give them control over everything they've lost. Clara... they think it's you."

Clara's grip tightened on the phone. She had always suspected that escaping The Ascendants wouldn't be easy. They had invested too much into their twisted plans to simply walk away. But she also knew one thing for sure—she was no longer afraid.

"I'm not running," Clara replied firmly. "If they want to come after me, they'll find out just how much power the Key of Unity really has."

Dr. Hart sighed, a note of admiration in her voice. "I expected nothing less from you. Just be careful. They're desperate now, and desperation can make people dangerous."

As she hung up the phone, Clara looked at Ethan, who had been listening silently by her side. He met her gaze, his expression resolute. "Whatever comes next, I'm with you, Clara. They won't get to you without going through me."

Clara felt a surge of gratitude and affection. She wasn't alone, and that knowledge gave her the courage to face whatever lay ahead.

Months passed, and though The Ascendants were quieter now, Clara remained vigilant. She continued to study her father's notes, learning everything she could about the Key of Unity and the power of resilience that it symbolized. Each day, she grew stronger, more certain of herself and the legacy her father had left behind.

One evening, as she and Ethan sat on her apartment's balcony, watching the sun dip below the horizon, Clara felt a sense of peace she hadn't known in years. The trials she had endured, the darkness she had faced—it all felt distant, like a shadow receding in the light.

Ethan reached over, taking her hand in his. "Do you ever wonder what's next for us?" he asked, a smile playing on his lips.

Clara looked at him, her own smile growing. "For the first time, I don't feel like I have to know. I think I just want to live, to enjoy every moment."

They sat together in silence, the warmth of his hand grounding her in the present. She knew there would always be challenges, that the world was full of those who sought power and control. But she also knew she had the strength to face whatever came her way, and that she had someone by her side who believed in her.

As the stars appeared overhead, Clara felt a quiet, unshakable resolve settle within her. She was no longer the girl defined by her father's secrets or The Ascendants' manipulation. She was Clara—the Key of Unity, a force of her own making.

And for the first time in her life, she was free.

The following months were marked by a strange calm that Clara embraced. The remnants of The Ascendants seemed to have scattered, but she remained cautious, knowing that some of them would never give up on regaining their lost influence.

Clara focused on building a new life for herself, one where she could finally explore her own ambitions and desires, free from the shadow of her father's secrets. She returned to her studies, found a job at a research institute, and began to consider how she might use her knowledge of the human mind to help others find freedom from trauma and manipulation.

One evening, she was preparing to meet Ethan for dinner when a letter arrived. The envelope was plain, bearing only her name and address in an elegant script. Her heartbeat quickened as she opened it, wondering if it might be a final message from The Ascendants or someone still loyal to their cause. Inside, she found a simple message, written in a familiar hand.

"The legacy lives on in you, Clara. Use it wisely."

There was no signature, but Clara knew the handwriting well—it was Dr. Hart's. A chill ran down her spine as she wondered what exactly Dr. Hart meant by "legacy." Had she also been a part of The Ascendants' twisted beliefs all along, or was she encouraging Clara to continue her father's path of resistance?

Clara folded the note, uncertainty swirling within her. She decided that whatever Dr. Hart's intentions, they didn't matter. The power of choice was hers alone now, and she would use it to shape her future on her own terms.

Later that night, Clara met Ethan at a small, cozy restaurant they often visited. As they enjoyed a quiet meal, she felt the weight of her journey lifting, replaced by a sense of renewal. She watched Ethan, his face relaxed and his laughter genuine, feeling grateful for his presence in her life. He had been her anchor through the storm, and she knew their bond had deepened in ways words could hardly describe.

As they left the restaurant, Ethan turned to her, his expression serious. "Clara, I want to talk to you about something important."

She raised an eyebrow, curious. "What is it?"

He took a deep breath, looking into her eyes. "I know we've been through a lot, and I know you're still finding your way. But... I can't imagine my life without you now. You've been my partner through everything, and I want us to keep building this life together."

Clara felt her heart swell, a smile breaking across her face. She hadn't anticipated the depth of her own feelings until now. For so long, she'd been focused on survival, but now, she realized that she wanted more than just freedom from the past—she wanted a future, and she wanted it with Ethan.

They stood together under the glow of the streetlights, wrapped in a silence that held all the unspoken promises between them.

"I want that too, Ethan," she said softly. "With you, I feel like I can finally be myself. No more hiding. No more shadows."

He took her hand, his grip warm and reassuring. They walked through the quiet streets, no words needed as they embraced the peace they'd fought so hard to find.

The next morning, Clara awoke with a renewed sense of purpose. She decided to take the journals and papers her father had left and turn them into something meaningful. Perhaps, she thought, she could write a book—a story of resilience, of breaking free from the chains of manipulation, told through her own experiences and her father's hidden legacy.

Ethan encouraged the idea, and together they spent countless nights organizing her father's notes, piecing together the fragments of his life's work. Clara wrote with an intensity she hadn't known she possessed, pouring her heart into each word, determined to share the lessons she had learned.

As the pages filled, she found herself healing, each chapter a step further from the shadows of The Ascendants and closer to her own light.

Months later, her book was complete. She titled it Unbound, a tribute to the journey she and her father had shared and to the freedom she had finally claimed. The book was more than a memoir—it was a testament to the power of choice, resilience, and unity.

To her surprise, Unbound resonated deeply with readers. People reached out to share how her story had given them the courage to confront their own pasts, to break free from cycles of fear and manipulation. Clara felt humbled, knowing that her father's legacy had transformed from a burden to a beacon of hope for others.

She also received a cryptic message from Dr. Hart once more, this time congratulating her on her book's success and hinting that her journey was only beginning. It was an eerie reminder that there were still forces at work in the world like The Ascendants, but Clara no longer feared them. She had faced the darkness and had come out stronger.

With Ethan by her side and her own voice guiding her, Clara was finally free to build a life filled with purpose, courage, and the love she had always yearned for.

And as she stood on the threshold of this new chapter, she knew that, whatever lay ahead, she would face it unbound, unafraid, and unbreakable.

In the months following the release of Unbound, Clara's life took on a new rhythm, one that was no longer punctuated by shadows lurking around every corner. Her book had become a quiet phenomenon, reaching readers across the globe and igniting conversations about resilience and freedom from toxic pasts. She began receiving invitations to speak at events, to share her story and help others find strength within themselves.

Though the thought of standing in front of large audiences filled her with apprehension, Ethan encouraged her, reminding her of all she had overcome. He stood by her side at each event, offering quiet words of support as she stepped into the spotlight, transforming from a survivor of darkness into a beacon of light for others.

One afternoon, after a speaking engagement, Clara was approached by a woman with familiar, piercing blue eyes. Her face was partially obscured by a hat, and she kept her gaze down, but Clara instantly felt a strange sense of recognition. The woman extended her hand, offering a faint smile.

"You may not remember me, Clara," she said, her voice low. "But I knew your father."

Clara's heart skipped a beat as memories of her father and The Ascendants surged back. She didn't know if this woman was friend or foe, but something compelled her to hear her out.

The woman introduced herself as Lillian, a former ally of her father who had worked in secret to dismantle the remnants of The Ascendants. She explained that after Daniel's defeat, a small faction of survivors had gone underground, intent on rising again with a more subtle, insidious influence.

"They've regrouped," Lillian said, her voice tense. "They're building something new—different from The Ascendants but just as dangerous. They call themselves The Eclipse now."

Clara's stomach twisted. She had hoped her struggle against the forces that had shaped her life was over, but it seemed the fight was far from finished. She looked at Lillian, wondering if she could trust her, but something in the woman's gaze told her that they shared a common enemy.

Lillian invited Clara to a private meeting, where a small group of former allies and survivors of The Ascendants gathered to discuss the growing influence of The Eclipse. Clara felt a strange sense of belonging among them, realizing that she wasn't alone in her determination to prevent another organization of control and manipulation from taking root.

At the meeting, they discussed the tactics The Eclipse had been using—underhanded partnerships, covert financial maneuvers, and quiet influence over public opinion. Unlike The Ascendants, The Eclipse was shrouded in secrecy, its leaders anonymous, and its agenda hidden behind layers of bureaucracy and misinformation.

Clara listened intently, her mind racing. She had thought her life would settle into normalcy, that she'd left her days of battling shadows behind. But now, she felt a new resolve forming within her.

"What can I do to help?" she asked, her voice steady.

Lillian smiled, as if she had been waiting for that question. "The same way you helped countless others with your book—by spreading the truth, by giving people the tools to see through manipulation and deception. You've already done it once, Clara. Now, we need you to do it again."

Clara returned home that night, her mind ablaze with ideas. The Eclipse's tactics were different from The Ascendants, more insidious and carefully hidden. She realized that to fight this new threat, she would need to shift her own approach as well.

With Ethan's help, she began researching deeper into the networks that The Eclipse had woven into society. They spent late nights pouring over articles, financial records, and obscure documents, connecting dots that most people would have missed. It was painstaking work, but Clara knew it was necessary.

As she dug deeper, she found disturbing evidence of The Eclipse's influence in media, politics, and corporate entities. They operated in plain sight, cloaked by the anonymity of modern society, exploiting people's fears and uncertainties to manipulate their beliefs and choices.

Driven by a fierce determination, Clara decided to write a series of articles, each one exposing a different layer of The Eclipse's operations. She was careful to back every claim with evidence, weaving her words with the same authenticity and courage that had made Unbound so powerful.

The articles began to gain traction, drawing the attention of both supporters and detractors. The public response was mixed; some praised her for exposing the truth, while others accused her of paranoia, claiming that she was fabricating conspiracy theories. But Clara remained undeterred, knowing that The Eclipse would do everything possible to discredit her.

One evening, as Clara was wrapping up her latest article, she received a chilling email from an anonymous sender. The message was short, but its implications were unmistakable.

"You've gone too far, Clara. Stop now, or face the consequences."

Clara felt a rush of fear but quickly steadied herself. She had expected retaliation, knowing that her fight against The Eclipse would come at a cost. But she also knew that she couldn't back down—not after all she had learned, and not after seeing the impact her words were beginning to have.

Ethan, who had been her constant support, encouraged her to continue, reminding her of the strength she had shown in the face of The Ascendants. He vowed to protect her, to stand by her side no matter the danger.

Together, they prepared for the fight ahead, knowing that it would take everything they had to bring The Eclipse's influence to light.

EIGHT

THE ARCHITECT REVEALED

Days turned into weeks, and the tension around Clara's life grew. Her articles had begun to uncover shocking revelations, linking key public figures to The Eclipse's web of influence. Each new revelation stirred public outrage and brought The Eclipse's operations further into the spotlight.

But Clara knew the battle was far from over. She could feel the eyes of powerful forces watching her every move, waiting for her to slip up. The sense of being followed, of unseen threats lurking in the shadows, became a constant in her life.

Then, one evening, as she and Ethan returned home, they found the door to her apartment slightly ajar. Her heart pounded as she pushed it open, revealing the wreckage within. Papers were scattered, her laptop smashed, and a single message was left scrawled on her wall in bold, red letters.

"Enough is enough."

Ethan clenched his fists, fury in his eyes. "They're trying to intimidate you, Clara. They want you to feel helpless."

But Clara, despite the fear gripping her, felt something stronger rise within her—defiance. The Eclipse might be powerful, but she refused to be silenced.

"This only means we're closer to the truth," she whispered. "They're desperate now."

With renewed determination, Clara contacted Lillian and the others in the resistance network. They decided to go underground, operating from a secure location, determined to keep The Eclipse at bay and continue their work undeterred.

Clara knew the road ahead would be treacherous, that each step she took would bring her closer to the edge. But she also knew that she was no longer alone. Together with Ethan, Lillian, and others who had endured and fought, she had allies and a cause worth fighting for.

As she prepared for the next phase of her battle against The Eclipse, she realized something profound: her father's legacy was not merely one of resistance—it was a legacy of hope, resilience, and the courage to fight for truth, no matter the cost.

For Clara, this was no longer just about survival. It was about ensuring that no one else would be forced to live in the shadows of manipulation and control. It was about creating a world where people could live free, unbound by fear.

And as she looked toward the unknown future, Clara knew she was ready—ready to face whatever darkness awaited her, armed with truth, conviction, and the knowledge that she was no longer fighting alone.

The next few weeks blurred into a haze of late nights, cryptic meetings, and tense planning. Clara, Ethan, and their allies had moved to a small, secluded safehouse on the outskirts of the city, a place where they could work without the prying eyes of The Eclipse watching their every move.

Their focus was clear: to dismantle The Eclipse's influence, piece by piece. Lillian had tapped into her network of former intelligence contacts, gathering information on The Eclipse's operations and funding sources. Every new discovery felt like peeling back the layers of a dark and endless onion; the deeper they went, the more twisted it became.

One night, as Clara sifted through encrypted emails, she stumbled upon a document detailing "Project Umbra," a covert operation that The Eclipse had planned to deploy within the coming months. The project's goal was to subtly manipulate public opinion, using media partnerships and fake grassroots campaigns to influence legislation and push their agenda.

The implications were terrifying. If Project Umbra succeeded, The Eclipse would be able to subtly control public narratives, shaping people's beliefs and decisions without them even realizing it.

"We need to expose this," Clara said, her voice barely a whisper as she looked at Ethan. "If they succeed with Project Umbra, they'll have the power to control the entire city—and eventually, maybe even more."

Ethan nodded, his eyes dark with resolve. "Then we have no time to waste."

In the following days, Clara and her team worked tirelessly, preparing to reveal Project Umbra to the public. They knew that the information had to be released in a way that would reach the masses quickly, before The Eclipse could suppress it. They strategized, working with underground media contacts and whistleblower networks to ensure that their story would go viral the moment it went live.

Meanwhile, Clara sensed the walls closing in. The Eclipse was aware of her activities, and she could feel their presence tightening around her. Strange cars began to appear outside their safehouse at odd hours, and cryptic messages were left in her inbox, each one more threatening than the last.

But Clara refused to give in to fear. She had come too far to back down now.

The night before they were set to publish the exposé, Clara received a video message from an unknown number. She hesitated, but curiosity and a sense of foreboding compelled her to watch.

The screen flickered to life, revealing a dimly lit room. A man sat with his back to the camera, his voice distorted, though Clara could still make out the chilling calm in his tone.

"You think you're doing the right thing, Clara," he said. "But you're out of your depth. Walk away now, or the people closest to you will pay the price."

Clara's blood ran cold, but her jaw clenched with determination. She wouldn't let them intimidate her—not when the stakes were so high.

The morning of the release, Clara felt a mix of nerves and anticipation. She and her team had taken every precaution, ensuring that once the story went live, it would be nearly impossible to take down. They had multiple sources ready to mirror the article, and key allies in the media were prepared to amplify it across various platforms.

At exactly noon, they hit "publish." The article went live, detailing Project Umbra in painstaking detail, supported by leaked documents, witness testimonies, and the full network of connections linking The Eclipse to powerful public figures.

The response was immediate. Within hours, the story spread like wildfire. News outlets began picking up on the revelations, interviews were scheduled, and social media erupted with shock and outrage. People demanded accountability, calling for investigations into every person and organization tied to The Eclipse.

But Clara knew this was only the beginning. The Eclipse wouldn't go down without a fight.

That evening, as she sat with Ethan in the safehouse, watching the story unfold, her phone buzzed with another anonymous message.

"Well played, Clara. But did you really think we'd make it this easy?"

She stared at the screen, a knot forming in her stomach. The fight was far from over.

Two days later, the repercussions of the article began to ripple outward. Public figures linked to The Eclipse either denied involvement or resigned under pressure. Investigations were launched, and Clara's story had sparked a movement, empowering people to seek transparency and resist manipulation.

Yet amid the victory, a sense of dread lingered. Clara felt as if she were constantly being watched. Small things—like her phone glitching, or her emails vanishing and reappearing—hinted at The Eclipse's continued influence. They had the resources to go underground and bide their time, waiting for the right moment to resurface.

One evening, Ethan returned to the safehouse with news. "Lillian wants to meet. She says she has a lead on one of The Eclipse's high-ranking members—someone who might be able to dismantle the organization from the inside."

Curious and eager, Clara agreed to go. They met Lillian in a dimly lit café on the outskirts of town. She wore a heavy coat, her face partially obscured by a scarf, her voice lowered to a whisper.

"I've found someone willing to cooperate," Lillian said. "A man named Marcus Hayes. He was one of The Eclipse's chief strategists. He says he's willing to expose their remaining operations, but he's demanding complete immunity in return."

Clara exchanged a look with Ethan, sensing the risk. This could be a trap—or it could be their best chance to finally dismantle The Eclipse.

"We'll meet him," Clara said, her voice firm. "But on our terms."

A week later, they arranged to meet Marcus Hayes at a discreet location. As Clara and Ethan waited, nerves on edge, the door opened and a man in a dark suit entered. He had sharp, calculating eyes, and an air of tension clung to him.

"Clara, Ethan," he greeted, extending his hand. "I assume you know what I can offer you."

Clara studied him, wary but curious. "You say you can take down The Eclipse. But why now?"

Marcus sighed, glancing away. "The organization I helped build has grown beyond my control. They're not just manipulating the public; they're taking steps to control governments, markets, and lives. I can't be part of this anymore."

Clara sensed his sincerity but knew that his motives were likely complex. "If you're willing to expose them, we'll work with you. But I want full transparency."

Marcus nodded. "Agreed. I'll give you everything I have. But remember, Clara, by taking this step, you're declaring open war on some of the most powerful people in the world. Are you ready for that?"

Clara's gaze didn't waver. "I've been fighting them my whole life. I'm ready for whatever comes next."

Over the following weeks, Marcus provided Clara's team with valuable intelligence. His insider knowledge revealed a complex network of operations, funding channels, and coded communications that The Eclipse used to avoid detection.

Clara and her team worked tirelessly, verifying each piece of information and publishing updates that continued to shock the public. They exposed hidden alliances, shell companies, and covert transactions, each one chipping away at The Eclipse's fortress of secrecy.

But the deeper they dug, the more dangerous it became. Threats escalated, and people close to Clara and Ethan began receiving messages warning them to distance themselves. Even Lillian, with all her connections, found herself facing increased surveillance and pressure to abandon the cause.

Still, Clara refused to stop. She knew this was bigger than herself or even The Eclipse; this was a fight to protect the freedom and truth of countless lives.

One evening, as she worked late into the night, a new message appeared on her computer screen:

"This is your final warning. Leave while you still can."

Clara took a deep breath, feeling a mix of fear and resolve. She knew that whatever lay ahead, she couldn't turn back now.

She was prepared to face whatever darkness awaited, determined to bring The Eclipse's shadowed empire crumbling down—one revelation at a time.

The pressure mounted each day, but Clara's resolve only strengthened. With each revelation they published, the public grew more outraged, and the government could no longer ignore the outcry. Independent investigations were launched, and high-profile figures were called to testify. The Eclipse, once a faceless force, was now exposed and vulnerable.

Yet Clara knew better than to celebrate too soon. She felt like she was playing a high-stakes game of chess against an invisible opponent, and she suspected that The Eclipse still had moves left to make.

One evening, Clara received a message from Marcus. "I've uncovered something you need to see. Meet me tomorrow night at our usual spot."

Clara's stomach twisted. Every instinct told her to be cautious, but Marcus had been their most valuable source, and if he had uncovered something crucial, she couldn't afford to ignore it.

The next night, Clara and Ethan arrived at the meeting location—a secluded warehouse on the outskirts of town. The air was thick with tension as they approached the building, the dim lights casting long shadows. They moved cautiously, scanning their surroundings for any signs of trouble.

Inside, they found Marcus waiting, his expression grim. He motioned for them to follow him deeper into the warehouse. They reached a small room where Marcus had set up a laptop displaying a series of encrypted files.

"This is it," he said, pointing to the screen. "These documents detail The Eclipse's final plan, one that goes far beyond controlling the public. They call it 'Project Dominion.' If they succeed, they'll be able to manipulate entire economies, governments, and even military operations—all from behind the scenes."

Clara's breath caught as she scrolled through the files. The extent of The Eclipse's ambitions was staggering. Project Dominion wasn't just about influence; it was about absolute control.

Ethan clenched his jaw, his fists balled. "We need to get this out to the public immediately. This is bigger than anything we've exposed so far."

Marcus nodded, but his expression remained wary. "They'll come for us all, Clara. Once we reveal this, there's no turning back."

Clara met his gaze, her voice steady. "Then we make sure it counts."

NINE

FRACTURING SHADOWS

The next 48 hours were a whirlwind of planning and coordination. Clara's team worked tirelessly to encrypt the files and prepare them for release. They knew they had to be strategic—Project Dominion was the type of revelation that could destabilize governments, and they had to handle it carefully.

As they finalized their plans, Clara received a sudden phone call. The voice on the other end was familiar, chillingly calm.

"You've taken this too far, Clara," the voice said. It was the same distorted tone she'd heard in previous warnings. "Project Dominion is beyond your comprehension. If you continue, we won't just come after you. Everyone you love will suffer."

The threat shook her, but she forced herself to remain calm. She knew The Eclipse's tactics by now—they thrived on fear, on using people's vulnerabilities against them. But Clara was done being intimidated.

She ended the call without responding, her resolve unshaken. This was no longer just a fight for truth; it was a battle for freedom, for the right to live without invisible strings dictating their lives.

The morning of the release, Clara's nerves were stretched to their limit. She barely slept, running on adrenaline as she and her team prepared to unleash Project Dominion's secrets. She knew they were taking a massive risk, that they could be facing repercussions far worse than threats. But they all understood the stakes.

At exactly noon, the exposé went live. The article was more than just a bombshell; it was a direct attack on The Eclipse's very foundation. Clara included detailed evidence of Project Dominion's goals, listing the powerful individuals and organizations involved. She made sure there was no room for doubt, no way for anyone to deny The Eclipse's intentions.

The response was immediate and overwhelming. News stations interrupted regular programming, experts and political figures weighed in, and social media erupted with calls for justice. Within hours, the story became a global phenomenon, sparking outrage and protests around the world.

For a brief, exhilarating moment, Clara felt victorious. But she knew The Eclipse wouldn't take this lying down.

That night, Clara and Ethan returned to the safehouse, exhausted but hopeful. They knew they had struck a significant blow, but Clara remained vigilant. She knew that The Eclipse, even in its most vulnerable state, was still dangerous.

As they settled in for a moment's rest, the lights flickered, and a strange silence filled the room. Ethan reached for his phone, only to find it dead, along with every other device in the room.

A sudden loud knock echoed from the door. Clara's heart raced as she and Ethan exchanged a look, their minds racing through the worst possibilities.

Without warning, the door burst open, and a group of masked figures entered, moving swiftly and purposefully. Clara barely had time to react before one of them grabbed her, pulling her to her feet.

"You were warned, Clara," one of the figures whispered, his voice a cold reminder of the threats she had ignored.

Ethan struggled, trying to break free from his captors, but Clara locked eyes with him, a silent message passing between them: Stay strong. Don't give up.

The last thing Clara saw before they blindfolded her was Ethan's face, his expression filled with both defiance and despair.

Hours passed, or perhaps only minutes—it was impossible to tell. Clara felt herself being dragged through unfamiliar hallways, her mind foggy from whatever they had used to sedate her.

Finally, the blindfold was removed, and she found herself in a dimly lit room, facing a man she recognized from her research. He was one of The Eclipse's top leaders, a shadowed figure with a carefully maintained public image.

He watched her with a cold, calculating smile. "You've caused us quite a bit of trouble, Clara. Did you really think you could take us down?"

Clara met his gaze, refusing to show any fear. "The truth is out there. People know who you are now. You can't hide anymore."

The man chuckled, unbothered. "Oh, we're more adaptable than you give us credit for. And people...they forget. They get distracted. Soon enough, this will all blow over, and we'll rebuild, stronger than ever."

Clara clenched her fists. She could see he believed every word he said, that The Eclipse was prepared to wait out the storm she had caused.

But she also knew she wasn't alone. The resistance, the public outcry—she had sparked something that couldn't be easily extinguished.

The man leaned closer, his voice soft and menacing. "But you, Clara, won't get the chance to see it."

She steeled herself, ready to face whatever fate awaited her, when suddenly a commotion erupted outside the room. Raised voices, footsteps pounding down the hall. Before she could comprehend what was happening, the door burst open.

Ethan appeared, flanked by members of Lillian's resistance team, their faces determined. The element of surprise was on their side, and they quickly overpowered Clara's captors.

In the chaos, Ethan reached Clara, pulling her to her feet. "Let's get out of here."

As they fled through the corridors, Clara felt a surge of hope. They had struck a blow to The Eclipse, weakened it in ways it hadn't anticipated. She realized now that their fight would be ongoing, that the shadows would always try to reclaim power.

But they had sparked a movement, and movements could spread like wildfire.

Back in the safety of the resistance's underground base, Clara took a deep breath, her mind racing with the events of the past few hours. She knew The Eclipse would regroup, that the fight was far from over.

But as she looked around at her allies—at Ethan, Lillian, and the countless others who had joined their cause—she felt a new sense of purpose.

"From here on, we don't just expose the truth," she said, her voice steady. "We give people the tools to see through the lies, to recognize the manipulation. We won't just fight the shadows; we'll empower others to see the light."

The room filled with determined nods, a shared understanding that their journey was only beginning.

As Clara prepared for the long road ahead, she felt a fierce, unbreakable resolve. The Eclipse might be powerful, but so was the truth—and she was prepared to fight for it, no matter the cost

Months passed, and the world seemed to settle into a tense equilibrium. The initial fury surrounding Project Dominion's exposure had simmered down, replaced by quiet murmurs of conspiracy and distrust. Clara had returned to her life, but it was a shadow of what it once was. She had new allies, a network of resistance, and a purpose that fueled her every waking moment.

Yet, the threat of The Eclipse lingered, ever-present, like a dark cloud on the horizon.

As Clara adjusted to the strange mix of vigilance and hope, whispers began to reach her—a possible sighting of The Eclipse's leader, a trail of unexplained disappearances, and financial shifts in secretive offshore accounts. Clara's gut told her that The Eclipse was laying low, gathering strength for a counterattack.

One night, as she sifted through a fresh batch of encrypted messages, a new name appeared in her research: "The Architect."

Rumored to be the original mind behind The Eclipse, The Architect's name struck fear into even the most seasoned of her sources. Clara's hands trembled slightly as she read more.

If this mysterious figure truly existed, then The Eclipse's ambitions weren't dead; they were only beginning.

The Architect's legend grew darker with each clue she uncovered. He was said to be a master of psychological manipulation, a strategist who designed The Eclipse's most insidious operations, but he had always remained in the shadows, letting others take the fall while he orchestrated everything from a distance.

Ethan warned Clara to be cautious. "This isn't just any enemy, Clara. If The Architect's as powerful as they say, he could manipulate everything around you without you even knowing."

But Clara couldn't shake the feeling that finding The Architect was the key to bringing down The Eclipse for good. She reached out to her contacts, combing through every connection and dark web database she could access, piecing together hints and fragments that pointed to The Architect's real identity.

Her search eventually led her to a small town outside the city, where one of her sources claimed The Architect had been sighted. It was a quiet, inconspicuous place—a fitting hiding spot for someone as elusive as he was.

Clara and Ethan arrived in the town at dawn, their nerves sharp as they blended in among the early risers and shopkeepers. Following her contact's directions, they walked through a maze of narrow alleyways and rundown buildings until they reached a modest, unremarkable house on the edge of town.

Clara's heart raced as they approached the door, feeling the weight of the moment. This could be it—the lead that would finally bring The Eclipse crashing down.

They knocked, and after a tense pause, the door creaked open. An older man with sharp, penetrating eyes stood in the doorway. He was calm, almost serene, as if he had been expecting them.

"You've come a long way to find me," he said, his voice smooth and unsettling.

Clara's breath caught. She knew, without a doubt, that she was face-to-face with The Architect.

v

Inside the dimly lit room, The Architect motioned for them to sit. Clara felt an unsettling calm as he spoke, his words measured and deliberate. He admitted to creating The Eclipse, to masterminding the operation from the shadows. But his tone was devoid of remorse, as if every choice he had made was perfectly justified.

"People are sheep, Clara," he said, his voice chillingly rational. "They need guidance—someone to show them the way, to shape them into something greater. That's what The Eclipse was meant to do. But people like you...you're a disruption. A threat to the order I've built."

Clara felt a surge of anger. "You're manipulating people's lives, controlling them without their knowledge. That's not order—it's tyranny."

The Architect's eyes glinted. "Tyranny is simply the price of progress. And you, Clara, are in way over your head."

She wanted to argue, to expose him as the monster he was, but he cut her off.

"You don't understand the scope of what you're up against. Destroy me, and another will rise. The Eclipse is not a person—it's an idea. And ideas are far harder to kill than men."

TEN

A NEW THREAT – PHOENIX

After hours of tense conversation, The Architect finally offered her a deal. "You have a choice, Clara," he said, his gaze steady. "Join me. Use your talents to shape the world in ways you never imagined. Or continue your foolish resistance and watch everything you love fall apart."

Clara was stunned. The man who had been her enemy for so long was offering her a place within his organization, an opportunity to wield the very power she had fought to expose.

Ethan, sensing her hesitation, shook his head. "Clara, don't listen to him. He's manipulating you."

But The Architect's voice was intoxicating, his promises wrapped in a twisted logic that held a dark appeal. In a world filled with chaos, he offered certainty—control. And for a fleeting moment, Clara wondered if he was right.

Yet, as she looked into his cold, calculating eyes, she knew she could never join him. She had seen the devastation The Eclipse had caused, felt the fear they instilled. To join him would be to betray everything she stood for.

She straightened, meeting his gaze. "I'll never join you."

The Architect's expression darkened. "Very well. But remember, Clara—no one defies The Eclipse and lives to tell about it."

As they left the house, Clara knew their lives would never be the same. The Architect had given her a glimpse into the darkness of his mind, and it terrified her to realize just how deeply The Eclipse's influence ran. But the encounter also solidified her resolve. She understood now that her fight was not just against The Eclipse, but against a mindset—a philosophy that valued control over freedom, power over humanity.

With renewed determination, Clara and Ethan returned to the resistance, sharing everything they had learned. They doubled their efforts, building alliances, and creating tools to educate the public on recognizing manipulation and resisting control.

Clara's message was clear: The Eclipse was not invincible. Its power lay in secrecy, in the shadows it cast, and by exposing its true nature, they could weaken it.

And somewhere, in the quiet hours of the night, Clara held onto a fragile hope—that maybe, just maybe, they could finally bring The Eclipse to an end.

Months passed, and the resistance grew stronger, their ranks filled with people inspired by Clara's courage. The public had become more vigilant, more questioning, and The Eclipse was no longer a faceless entity; it was a symbol of oppression, of secrets kept in the dark.

One evening, as Clara sat reviewing intel, she received a message on her encrypted line. It was from an anonymous source who claimed to have information on The Eclipse's final plan—a desperate, all-or-nothing move to regain control and silence their opponents once and for all.

The message was brief, but its implications were chilling. It read: "They're coming for you. Be ready."

Clara's heart pounded, but she was no longer afraid. She had seen the darkest depths of her enemy, and she knew that the only way to defeat them was to confront them head-on.

As she prepared for the battle ahead, she knew that this fight—this choice to resist, to stand against the shadows—was one she was willing to make, no matter the cost.

The resistance mobilized quickly. Clara's team fortified their safehouses, encrypted their communications, and reached out to allies across the country. They knew that The Eclipse would strike soon, and Clara refused to be caught off guard. Every night, she trained alongside her team, honing skills she'd once thought she'd never need.

The Architect's message echoed in her mind: "They're coming for you." It was a promise as much as it was a threat.

Late one evening, Clara received an unexpected message on her personal device. It was a live video feed, and as it loaded, she recognized the face immediately: her younger brother, Alex, tied to a chair, surrounded by masked figures.

A voice, cold and taunting, came through the feed. "You thought you could fight us and win, Clara? We warned you. Now, it's time for you to make a choice."

The feed went black, and her device pinged with a message: "Come alone if you want to save him."

Ethan tried to convince Clara not to go. "This is exactly what they want, Clara. It's a trap. They know you'll walk into it."

But Clara's mind was set. She couldn't abandon her brother, not after everything The Eclipse had taken from her already. She armed herself, taking only the essentials, and left a message with Ethan: "If I don't come back, promise me you'll keep fighting."

As she left the safehouse, her mind raced through every possible scenario. She knew she was walking into a trap, but she also knew that The Eclipse underestimated her. They thought fear would break her, but she was fueled by something far stronger—resolve.

Following the cryptic instructions, Clara arrived at an abandoned factory on the outskirts of the city. The silence was suffocating as she crept inside, every shadow seeming to watch her.

After a few tense minutes, she spotted her brother, still tied up, his face pale and exhausted. Relief washed over her, but she remained cautious. She knew The Eclipse wouldn't leave him unguarded.

Suddenly, a figure stepped out from the shadows—it was The Architect himself, his expression unreadable. He held up a small device, his finger poised over a button. "You've caused me more trouble than I expected, Clara."

Clara's voice was steady as she replied. "Let him go. This is between you and me."

The Architect's lips curled into a smile. "You're right. But I want you to understand something." He gestured to her brother. "He's collateral. Your choices led us here, Clara. You made this happen."

Clara gritted her teeth. "No, you did. And I won't let you use innocent people to keep control."

Without warning, Clara lunged forward, her movements precise and quick. The Architect's guards sprang into action, but Clara fought with a ferocity born of desperation. She struck with calculated strength, her training paying off as she took down the first two guards. But more surrounded her, and soon, she was overwhelmed.

Just as she felt herself being restrained, a loud crash echoed through the room. Ethan and members of the resistance stormed in, taking The Architect's men by surprise. A full-scale fight erupted, and amidst the chaos, Clara managed to break free, rushing to untie Alex.

As the sounds of gunfire and shouts filled the air, Clara looked up to see The Architect slipping away in the confusion. She caught his eye for a brief moment—a look of cold fury and resentment.

But she didn't chase him. Her focus was on Alex, who clung to her, his face pale but alive. "We're getting out of here," she whispered, her voice fierce with determination.

They made it out of the factory just as it began to collapse, the sounds of explosions echoing behind them. Clara, Ethan, and the resistance members piled into waiting vehicles, speeding away before The Eclipse could regroup.

Back at their hideout, Clara held Alex close, feeling a weight lift off her shoulders. But she knew this wasn't over. The Architect was still out there, more determined than ever to see her destroyed.

As dawn broke, Clara sat with Ethan, her mind racing. "We need to take this fight to the next level," she said quietly. "We can't just react to them anymore. We have to dismantle them at the root."

Ethan nodded, a steely resolve in his eyes. "Then let's finish what we started."

Over the following weeks, Clara's team launched their most aggressive campaign yet. They targeted The Eclipse's funding sources, exposed key players, and rallied support from whistleblowers. Governments and private organizations joined the resistance, finally understanding the true scope of The Eclipse's operations.

But Clara knew that until The Architect himself was brought down, The Eclipse would never truly die. She and her team pursued every lead, following the faintest trail until they reached The Architect's private estate—a heavily fortified mansion hidden in a secluded forest.

It was a risky mission, but Clara was done playing it safe.

Under cover of night, Clara, Ethan, and a select team infiltrated the estate. Moving through the shadows, they disabled security systems and avoided patrols. Each step brought them closer to The Architect, closer to ending this once and for all.

Finally, they reached his study—a grand room filled with relics of power and control. The Architect sat behind a large desk, as if waiting for them.

He looked at Clara with a mixture of disdain and admiration. "You're persistent, I'll give you that. But you're also predictable."

With a subtle hand gesture, he activated hidden defenses, and the room's doors locked. Guards flooded in, and Clara's team braced for a fight.

But this time, Clara had anticipated his tricks. With a signal, backup teams outside the estate launched a diversion, drawing away most of The Architect's security forces. Clara and Ethan engaged The Architect's guards, their movements precise and relentless.

The Architect, realizing he was cornered, attempted to flee, but Clara intercepted him, blocking his path.

ELEVEN

RISING FROM THE ASHES

The two faced off, their eyes locked in a silent battle of wills. The Architect sneered, his voice dripping with contempt. "You think you've won? Even if you kill me, The Eclipse will rise again. Ideas don't die, Clara."

Clara shook her head. "Maybe not, but people like you—people who think they can control everyone else—they're replaceable. And it's time to end your reign."

With a final, decisive move, Clara subdued The Architect, securing him for capture. She could see the fear in his eyes, the realization that he had lost.

As they escorted him out, Clara felt a profound sense of closure. The man who had haunted her for so long, who had caused so much destruction, was finally defeated.

Back at the resistance base, news of The Architect's capture spread quickly, sparking celebrations. Clara watched her team, their faces lit with joy and relief, and she allowed herself a rare moment of peace. They had done the impossible, taking down an organization that had once seemed invincible.

But she knew that the fight wasn't truly over. The Eclipse's ideas still lingered, woven into systems of power and control across the world. She made a vow to continue her work, to keep exposing corruption and empowering people to resist manipulation.

As she looked out over her team, she felt a quiet pride. They had become more than just a resistance; they were a force for change, a reminder that even in the darkest times, there were those willing to stand up and fight.

And in that moment, Clara realized that her journey, though far from over, had only just begun.

In the weeks following The Architect's capture, Clara's world was transformed. The Eclipse's leadership was fractured, its influence waning as whistleblowers and former insiders came forward. Media outlets worldwide were filled with reports on the inner workings of the organization, exposing years of corruption, manipulation, and control. Public outrage surged, and allies of The Eclipse, once untouchable, found themselves facing consequences for their actions.

Yet, for Clara, it was a strange, bittersweet victory. She had won, yes, but the fight had cost her dearly. The people she had lost, the lives that had been upended—they weighed heavily on her heart.

One evening, as she sat alone in her office, her phone buzzed. She glanced at the screen and saw a message from an unknown number: "Meet me. I have information."

Normally, she would have ignored such cryptic messages, but something about this one felt... familiar. Against her better judgment, she decided to investigate.

Clara found herself at a secluded café on the edge of town, her instincts on high alert. She chose a seat by the window, where she could see anyone approaching. Minutes passed, and just as she was about to leave, a man slid into the seat across from her.

Her eyes widened in shock. It was Liam—a friend from her past, someone she had thought lost in the chaos of The Eclipse's rise. He looked older, wearier, but his eyes held the same intensity she remembered.

"Liam," she whispered, barely believing her eyes. "You're alive?"

He nodded, a faint smile tugging at his lips. "Barely. I had to disappear for a while... but I never stopped watching, Clara."

Before she could respond, he slid a thin file across the table. "You may have taken down The Eclipse, but there's more to this story than you know. There are still players in the shadows, people who profited from The Eclipse but kept their hands clean. They're still out there, working on a new project—one they call 'Phoenix.'"

Clara's heart sank. She had hoped The Eclipse's defeat would bring an end to the darkness, but it seemed there were more layers, more threats lurking just beneath the surface.

Liam explained that Phoenix was a plan to reestablish control, but in a more insidious way. Instead of outright manipulation, it aimed to subtly influence people through advanced technologies—smart devices, media algorithms, even artificial intelligence.

"The Architect was just one part of a much larger machine," Liam said, his voice filled with urgency. "Phoenix is different. It's designed to look harmless, even helpful. But it's the same agenda—control, influence, power. And now that The Eclipse is exposed, they're planning to roll it out even faster."

Clara's mind raced as she processed his words. She realized that Phoenix represented an even greater threat than The Eclipse because it didn't rely on fear or intimidation; it relied on trust. People would willingly embrace it, never knowing they were being manipulated.

"We can't let this happen," she said, her voice resolute.

Liam nodded. "I knew you'd feel that way. That's why I came to you. You've already proven you can dismantle the seemingly invincible. Now... you just have to do it again."

As they left the café, Clara felt the familiar fire reignite within her. This new battle would be different, more subtle, but no less dangerous. Phoenix was a specter that could infiltrate every part of society, undetected by those it influenced.

Clara knew she needed to adapt her approach. She couldn't rely on traditional methods; Phoenix required new tactics, new allies, and a deeper understanding of the technology it used. She and Liam spent hours strategizing, mapping out the connections and hidden ties that linked Phoenix to influential companies, government agencies, and tech giants.

They reached out to experts—hackers, data analysts, journalists—who could help them expose Phoenix's agenda. Slowly, they began to piece together the puzzle, identifying key players and uncovering hidden funding streams.

The deeper Clara dug, the more dangerous the mission became. Phoenix was protected by layers of secrecy, and its operatives were as cunning as they were ruthless. Clara and her team faced constant threats—surveillance, smear campaigns, even attempts to discredit them publicly. But they pressed on, refusing to be silenced.

One night, as Clara worked late, she received a call from Ethan. "Clara, you need to see this," he said, his voice laced with urgency.

He sent her a video clip—footage of a politician she had long suspected of being involved with Phoenix. The clip revealed the politician's direct involvement in Phoenix's agenda, discussing plans to subtly shape public opinion through social media and entertainment.

It was the breakthrough they needed.

Despite the victories, Clara knew the fight wasn't over. Phoenix's core leaders were still at large, and they would do everything in their power to rebuild. But she had faith in her team, in the allies they had gained, and in the resilience of those who refused to be controlled.

One night, as she stood on a rooftop overlooking the city, she felt a profound sense of purpose. The journey had changed her, shaped her into someone who understood both the darkness and the light within herself.

This fight was no longer just about taking down an organization—it was about preserving humanity's freedom, its ability to choose, to think, and to resist.

With Liam, Ethan, and countless others by her side, Clara knew that no matter how many times shadows tried to rise, she would be there, ready to stand against them.

And for the first time in a long time, she felt hope—not just for herself, but for everyone who believed in the power of truth.

Afterword

Writing The Shadow of Control was an exploration of modern power dynamics and the profound impact of unseen influence on society. As Clara's journey reveals, standing against invisible forces requires resilience, courage, and an unwavering belief in the truth. In an age where control is often wielded quietly, this story is a reminder that questioning, investigating, and confronting shadowy powers remain essential. Thank you for joining Clara and her team on this journey—we hope her story leaves you inspired to seek the truth in your own way.

Author's Note

The Shadow of Control is a work of fiction, though it draws inspiration from the realities of our interconnected world. The characters, organizations, and events depicted are fictional; however, the themes of power, influence, and autonomy are deeply rooted in contemporary issues. We encourage readers to reflect on the questions this book raises and to consider how similar dynamics might impact their own lives. Above all, we hope this story sparks thought, discussion, and perhaps a bit of the courage needed to stand up for the truth.

Glossary

The Eclipse – A covert organization seeking to control global narratives and influence society's choices from the shadows.

The Architect – The enigmatic leader of The Eclipse, whose grand vision of control is thwarted by Clara and her allies.

Phoenix – A successor project to The Eclipse, aiming to use subtle, technologically enhanced means of control rather than overt manipulation.

www.ingramcontent.com/pod-product-compliance
Lightning Source LLC
Chambersburg PA
CBHW031446150726
47990CB00007B/2625